Ollinger said, "There's no call for trouble between us, Norwood."

Norwood gave him a brittle smile. "There needn't be any, Matt, but somebody stole a bunch of Colonel Judkins' steers up north. I'm checking this herd for them."

Ollinger's hand edged back toward the six-shooter that rested in a greasy holster at his hip. It lifted quickly again as Norwood's knuckles whitened against his saddle gun.

"You'll find no Judkins' cattle here," Ollinger gritted.

"Maybe not. But we're going to look."

Color squeezed into Ollinger's face. "Nobody's cutting this herd. I got six men here, besides myself. You can't buck seven of us, Norwood. Not alone."

Norwood said, "I'm not alone." He pointed his chin northward.

Ollinger turned in the saddle, then stiffened. Down from a low ridge eight men came riding. Eight men, riding abreast. Even through the restless dust, it was easy to tell that they were well-armed.

Yes, Matt Ollinger had a reputation. Man with nerves like rawhide, they said. Fearless. A killer.

But Espy Norwood could smell the fear that rose in the man, that rippled just beneath the skin. And he knew the reputation for what it was—a hoax.

Charter Westerns by Elmer Kelton

HOT IRON

BY ELMER KELTON

CHARTER BOOKS, NEW YORK

HOT IRON

A Charter Book / published by arrangement with
the author

PRINTING HISTORY
First Charter edition / July 1979
Second printing / December 1984
Third printing / June 1986

For information address: The Berkley Publishing Group,
200 Madison Avenue, New York, New York 10016.

ISBN: 0-441-34337-6

Charter Books are published by The Berkley Publishing Group,
200 Madison Avenue, New York, New York 10016.
PRINTED IN THE UNITED STATES OF AMERICA

HOT IRON

I

Espy Norwood found Matt Ollinger's herd just about the way he had figured he would. He put his horse down the gentle slope in an easy trot and rode in toward the railroad shipping pens. His bay horse shied off like a raw bronc and rolled its nose excitedly at the steaming locomotive which waited there, a tendril of coal smoke spiraling up from its high smokestack into the open Kansas sky. A long string of stock cars stretched out behind it on the cinder-stained spur track.

Norwood edged his horse through the shadow of the tall water tower and circled around the sprawling railroad pens. Five years under the blazing sun had bleached the raw color from the rough-sawed lumber and left it a leaden gray.

Spring grass inside the pens had made its full growth and now was curing under the summer sky, undisturbed by trampling hoofs. These out-of-the-way pens were not used much, Norwood observed. That would be Ollinger's reason for bringing the cattle here.

Beyond the corrals Norwood saw what he had expected, a dusty veil hovering brown over a bunched-up herd of rangy cattle. There was little bawling. Had there been, the easy drift of the earth-warm breeze would have carried it to him. No, this was a quiet bunch, a steer herd.

Norwood stood in his stirrups, squinting his gray eyes to count the men who ringed the cattle. Dressed in saddle-worn, brush-ripped range clothes with the dust and grime rubbed deep into the fabric, he was a medium-tall man with back as straight as the barrel of a Winchester. His unshaven chin set rigid and grave. His uncompromising gray eyes right now were blunt as bullet ends. He looked his thirty-five years and more, a man on whom the years had burned a deep brand.

With one quick glance behind him, he reached down and pulled the saddle gun out of its scabbard. He loaded it, placed it across the pommel in front of him, and gently touched spurs to the bay's grain-swelled sides. Out yonder, on the near side of the herd, he saw the man he wanted.

Warily watching the riders who held the herd, Norwood nevertheless let his eyes search over the gathering of steers. They were stockman's eyes, appraising the cattle out of long habit and the knowledge accumulated through years on horseback. These were Texas stock, not what the settlers called "American cattle." They were long of leg and horn, and sprinkled with every color a beef animal could have. Likely they had come up the trail from Texas the year before and spent the winter on a northern range. They didn't carry the flesh that a full summer would give them. But they were fat enough to do.

Norwood's gaze searched over the brands he saw on the rangy hips and stretchy sides. He pulled up short at the sight of one. It was meant to be a cloverleaf. For the time it takes to draw a deep breath, Norwood's gray eyes narrowed with the promise of anger.

Burnt cattle, he thought.

Then he edged away again, eyes leveling on the man who rode out to meet him.

Matt Ollinger reined up so that his horse and Norwood's were touching heads. Ollinger was a heavy-shouldered man with a bristly black beard sprinkled gray by dust, and with washed-out eyes that seemed to look through a man. His hostile gaze dropped to Norwood's saddle gun.

Its muzzle pointed at his stomach.

His expression never altered. He cupped huge hands over the high horn of his saddle.

"We're grown men, Norwood," he said evenly. "There's no reason for us to pretend anything to each other. I don't like you and you don't like me. I'm working cattle here. I'd be much obliged if you just kept a-riding."

Espy Norwood leaned forward, his hand tight on the saddle gun. "I figure on doing a little cattle work myself. With *these* cattle."

Ollinger's eyes were bottomless pools. His hands eased backward on the saddle horn. He bore a hard name, and he knew it better than anyone. The name Matt Ollinger brought a quiver of fear to many men. There were five notches on his gun, some said. Others declared it was more.

Ollinger said, "There's no call for trouble between us, Norwood."

Norwood gave him a brittle smile. "There needn't be any, Matt. But somebody stole a bunch of Colonel Judkins' steers up north. I'm checking this herd for them."

Ollinger's hand edged back toward the six-shooter that rested in a greasy holster at his hip. It lifted quickly again as Norwood's knuckles whitened against his saddle gun.

"You'll find no Judkins cattle here," Ollinger gritted.

"Maybe not. But we're going to look."

Color squeezed into Ollinger's face. "Nobody's cutting this herd. I got six men here, besides myself. You can't buck seven of us, Norwood. Not alone."

Norwood said, "I'm not alone." He pointed his chin northward.

Ollinger turned in the saddle, then stiffened. Down from a low ridge eight men came riding. Eight men, riding abreast. Even through the restless dust, it was easy to tell that they were well-armed.

Yes, Matt Ollinger had a reputation. Man with nerves like rawhide, they said. Fearless. A killer.

But Espy Norwood could smell the fear that rose in the man, that rippled just beneath the skin. And he knew the reputation for what it was—a hoax.

Norwood said, "Four hundred and fifty head, maybe five hundred, the colonel lost off of his winter range in Wyoming. You took them, Matt. You didn't know it, but we've watched you. We let you winter them, let you drive them down here.

"You were afraid to risk loading them at Dodge, where somebody might take too close a look. So you picked this place."

Ollinger shook his head. "You're wrong, Norwood. All wrong."

Norwood's eight men had reached the herd. They scattered, one man reining up beside each of Ollinger's men. Espy could see the guns drop. The two extra riders jogged around to Norwood. One of them pointed his long jaw toward the cattle.

"That cloverleaf or whatever it is—looks to me like somebody took a running iron to the JB Connected that was on them Texas steers the colonel bought last fall."

Norwood nodded. "That's the way I saw it. Rope one out, Tommy. We'll make sure."

Tommy Jensen shook down his rope and settled the loop around the horns of a rangy, mottley-faced steer. The steer crow-hopped, slinging his head and fighting the rope as the cowboy dragged him away from the other cattle. The second man roped the steer's heels. They stretched him out.

Kneeling on the steer's side, Jensen fingered the brand, peering closely at it. He looked up, frowning. "Hard to tell, Espy."

"If the brand's been altered, it'll show under the hide. Shoot him."

Ollinger exploded. "Them's *my* cattle, Norwood. Kill one and I'll have the marshal on you."

Norwood said evenly, "If we're wrong, we'll pay you for him. If we're right . . ."

He let it hang there. Ollinger's jaw ridged under a dirt-crusted beard.

Tommy Jensen aimed at the base of the steer's horns. The animal jerked and fell limp. Jensen skinned down a big flap of hide, exposing the back side of the brand. He swore gently, then cut off the piece of hide.

"You don't owe him a nickel, Espy."

Norwood's eyes hardened. He reached into his pocket and pulled out a small book. "How many steers in this herd, Matt?"

Ollinger hesitated. "Seven hundred and thirty."

Norwood handed him the book and a stub pencil, keeping one hand on the saddle gun all the time.

"Write out a bill of sale to the colonel. Seven hundred and thirty steers."

Ollinger's eyes crackled. He hurled the book to the ground. "You can't get away with this. I know you, Espy Norwood. You're nothing but a sodden, whisky-soaked . . ."

The butt of Norwood's saddle gun struck him across the mouth. The sound of it was like the breaking of a dry mesquite stick. Ollinger tumbled from the saddle, landing in a heap. Groggily he struggled to his knees, the blood trickling down his beard in a crooked, dirty line.

"Get up, Matt," Norwood breathed. Slowly Ollinger got to his feet, his face aflame. He flexed his gun hand, weighing his chances.

But he saw something in Norwood's eyes, something that stopped him. He saw death pushing hard against a restraining will.

And Ollinger's counterfeit metal crumbled before the keen steel of Norwood's stare. His shoulders slumped. He reached down and picked up the book where it had fallen. He took the pencil and began to scrawl.

Norwood reached into his pocket and withdrew two gold pieces. "Make it for ten dollars and considerations," he said.

In a minute Ollinger handed him the book. Norwood pitched the coins to the ground at his feet.

Futile anger rippling in his face, Ollinger asked, "What about the considerations?"

Norwood stared levelly at him. "The considerations are that we don't leave you hanging from that water tower yonder. We ought to. Now take your men and get away from here, Matt."

Ollinger looked at the steers, his shoulders sagging in defeat. Six months he had spent working up to this day. Now he had lost everything in six minutes. Frustration and anger darkened his face. But outweighing them was the realization that he was whipped. "All right, Norwood," he spoke quietly, rubbing his mouth where blood still trickled, and a deep blue splotch was growing. "But there'll be another time."

"There'd better not be," Norwood told him. "Next time, I'll kill you."

II

COLONEL WALTER JUDKINS'S outer office was a reflection of the man himself. Expansive and comfortable. Just well enough kept to prevent it from looking disreputable. It was one place in this crazy, sprawling Kansas City where a man just in off the prairie and the smoky cattle trains could stretch out and feel halfway at ease.

Espy Norwood slacked on a well-stuffed divan, waiting, his legs crossed. He was clean-shaven now, and the shave had taken much of the hard look from him. He could still smell the soap from the hotel bath. He wore a new-bought shirt, its clean collar a gleaming white against the walnut brown of his skin.

His gray eyes leisurely roamed over the familiar room. A great man for books, the colonel was. All around the place, broad shelves bulged with them. And between the shelves, framed pictures covered up the walls. The old colonel's love of livestock showed in most of them. Here was a painting of a Thoroughbred stallion, unlike any real horse that ever lived. Yonder was a glorified version of a Durham bull pawing sand, his huge head lowered in lusty challenge.

And there in the center, over the heavy mahogany desk, hung the framed U.S. Army commission which had carried the colonel through from Shiloh and Gettysburg to the finish at Appomattox, a long time ago. Directly above that yellowing piece of paper were the portraits of Abraham Lincoln and Ulysses S. Grant, joined in a single gilded frame.

Time was when such as that would have set the blood aboil in many a Texas man. But Espy Norwood was long since used to it and accepted it in stride. He had been but a gangling boy when the war was fought. His father had ridden off with the men of the gray, leaving Espy to take care of a mother and six little brothers and sisters. Biggest job he had was to burn the Norwood brand on the increase from the cattle herd each year, and to keep the Norwood cattle from scattering all over the coastal country of South Texas, as other war-neglected herds were doing.

He had done a good job of it, for a kid. But by the time his father came riding hime with an empty sleeve and an age far beyond his years, the cattle weren't worth the powder it would take to shoot them. The family's shack was small, and the larder was smaller. So Espy Norwood rolled his scant belongings into a warbag and set forth to forage for himself. He had become a wandering, homeless kid in a land of wandering, homeless people, a restless people, aggressive, proud in poverty, never admitting defeat.

A loud argument was shaking the thin walls of Colonel Judkins's inner office. Espy knew it was none of his business, but he couldn't help hearing it, even through the closed door. He easily recognized the old colonel's thundering voice.

"You've made a profit every year, gentlemen. Not always a big profit, but a profit, at least. The way I see it, you haven't got any kick coming."

The answer snapped back in a sharp, piercing voice that Espy knew came from somewhere far east. "The Great Plains Land and Cattle Company came up with a twenty per cent return for its investors last year. Our syndicate made only five per cent. We're being cheated, Colonel. And we're going to put a stop to it."

Espy could almost hear the colonel's sudden, sharp intake of breath. "Slagel, are you trying to say that I've been cheating you?"

The answer was as cold and unwavering as a steel blade. "Perhaps you, Colonel, perhaps someone else. But we're being cheated."

An angry hand flung the office door open. The colonel stood there stiffly, his arm outstretched. "Get out, Slagel. Get out before I take a horsewhip to you."

The man named Slagel walked out, holding a soft fedora in his long hands and a cane under his arm. He was a tall, spidery man with a sharp, malevolent face that matched his voice. He was immaculately dressed in long, closely-tailored black coat and gray striped trousers which broke correctly across his expensive shoes.

He was followed by another, much shorter, man dressed in much the same manner, a self-important little man whose own indignation seemed to be merely a careful copy of Slagel's.

Slagel stopped and faced the colonel again. "We have better and safer investments for our money, Judkins. We will be more than happy to pull out of your wild scheme."

The portly colonel stood there with his short beard bristling. "Let me remind you, sir, that you signed binding contracts."

"Those contracts protected us as well as bound us, Colonel. One sign of fraud anywhere will relieve us of obligation. And mark my word, Judkins, we'll find fraud. Next month I'm going to take a group of our directors and attorneys to that ranch. If we find anything amiss, Colonel, you'll answer for it. We'll pull our money out of that company—every last dime!"

Espy had gotten to his feet as the men came out of the

office. He stood in front of the outer door, anger net-
tling him. Nobody had the right to accuse the colonel of
fraud.

Slagel noticed Espy for the first time. Fixing a hostile
gaze upon him, he slipped the cane from under his
arm. He pointed it at Espy, making a quick, sideward
motion with it.

"Step aside there," he ordered sharply.

A stubborn thrust of anger made Espy hold back a
moment, glaring. Then he eased to one side just enough
that Slagel could edge by. The shorter man followed
closely with a frowning glance at Espy.

Colonel Judkins walked up to the door and slammed
it after the men, slammed it so hard that the picture
frames rattled against the wall. He stood a moment,
staring at the closed door, his fists clenched. Then some
of the angry color drained from his full face. He turned
to Espy, forcing a weak smile that quickly died. "Hello, Espy." He grasped the range man's rough hand in
his own, his left hand on Espy's arm. "I've been
expecting you, Espy. Sorry you had to come at a time
like this."

He looked out the open window toward the stockyards, from which came drifting the sound of bawling
cattle. "Been a hard day, Espy. I need a drink."
Worriedly he glanced at the man with the saddle-
warped frame. "Would it bother you if I took one?"

Espy shook his head, a slow smile on his face. "It's
been a year since I had the last one, Colonel. Go right
ahead. It won't bother me."

Tiredly Colonel Judkins walked into his inner office.
He reached into a heavy cabinet and took out two
bottles. He studied them intently, then decided upon
one with a firm nod of his gray head. He put the other
one back and poured a healthy-sized drink into a glass.
He downed it, his face tightening, then relaxing slowly.

"Funny," he observed, "how different this stuff can be for different people. For some, like you, it's poison. For some, like me, it's a real tonic." He strode to his desk and picked up a small cedar box. He opened the lid and held the box out for Espy. "Straight from Havana."

Espy took one, and the colonel got one for himself. He bit the end off and missed the spittoon with it by a foot and a half. He struck a sulphur match on the underside of the expensive mahogany desk and drew long and hard until the end of the cigar began to glow. He flipped the smoking match at the spittoon and missed again.

He savored the cigar a moment, his anger slowly dwindling away. A mild pleasure tugged upward at the corners of his gray-shot beard, which he kept clipped in the style of Ulysses S. Grant. "How's your son getting along, Espy?" he asked after a bit.

Espy Norwood's face tightened suddenly. "Well, I guess. I haven't been to see him yet."

"Good kid. Nine years old now, isn't he?"

"Ten."

The colonel smiled ironically. "That's the trouble when you start getting old. Every time you turn around, there's another year gone." He fished in his pocket and brought out a silver dollar. "When you see him, Espy, give him this for me."

Then the colonel's face was serious again. "That was quite a stroke you pulled off with Matt Ollinger out there. Everybody on the Kansas City yards had the story inside of a day."

Seated, Espy Norwood drew thoughtfully on his cigar, not answering. The colonel went on.

"Worries me, though. Matt Ollinger has a hard name."

A deep frown darkened Espy's square face. "A

name given to him by men he's managed to buffalo. He's a four-flusher, a bluffer.''

"Sometimes it's the coward who's the most dangerous.''

Espy nodded. "I know. Might be I ought to've killed him.''

Pensively the colonel rolled the cigar around in his mouth. "I'm glad you didn't. Somebody else will, in due time. There's no reason it should be us. I had enough of that a long time ago, Espy.''

"I know, sir.''

An uneasy silence hovered about the colonel then. *Now's the time to tell him*, Espy thought. But after all these years, he dreaded it, and he held back.

The thought struck Espy that the old man had aged a lot in the months since he had last seen him. Certainly the worry lines in his high forehead had pinched a little deeper, and a broodiness had taken the old spark out of the coffee-bean brown of his eyes.

"Espy," Colonel Judkins spoke abruptly, looking out the window again, "how would you like to go back to Texas?''

Espy straightened. His first reaction was a quick warmth of pleasure. It had been a long time. "Some cattle you want bought down there?''

The colonel still faced the window, his wrinkled hands clasped behind his black coat and the cigar smoke forming a soft cloud over his head. "Not this time, Espy. This job is bigger. I want you to save me from going bankrupt!'' The old man turned to see Espy's jaw drop with surprise. "Yes, Espy, that's what I said. Bankrupt.''

Espy's hands seemed to weaken, and the cigar lost its taste. Bankrupt. He'd seen other big speculators like the colonel go that way. But somehow the colonel was something special. Espy had never seriously consid-

ered that it could happen to the old man. He winced at
a genuine touch of pain. The colonel was a good Yan-
kee.

Pointing his chin at the outer door, Espy asked, "Is
that what the argument was all about?"

The colonel nodded, sinking his heavy frame into a
leather-covered chair. Judkins's worried brown eyes
fastened themselves on Espy's. "You remember the
ranch I helped an English syndicate to buy a half interest in? The Figure 4 outfit down below the Cana-
dian?

"Well, there may not be anything wrong, Espy. It
may be just imagination. But on the other hand, there
may be a lot wrong. You've got to find out for me.
Safest deal in the world, it looked like when we went
down there. A broad, open, new grassland in the Texas
Panhandle. Good country, good as you'll find anywhere on the Staked Plains. Frank Bowman had gotten
there among the first, and he had taken over lots of
land. He had good cattle, and he had the reputation of
being a good manager. But he needed cash for one
reason or another, and the syndicate was in the heat to
invest some English capital. So we bought in with
Bowman.

"But we haven't made as much money as they
thought we ought to. You know how it is. All over
Europe, promoters have been painting a bright green
picture about all the money that's to be made in the cow
business. Like that stuff about the Great Plains Land
and Cattle Company. Twenty per cent. Horsefeathers!

"Now Slagel's a New York lawyer for the syndicate,
and he's found some new scheme he wants to sink the
syndicate money into. But he can't get at it if he can't
pull out of the Figure 4. He's fanned up a lot of unrest
among the stockholders. When he hits that ranch next
month, he'll go over it with a fine-tooth comb. He'd

give his right arm to find something I can't explain."

His brown eyes were clouded with worry. "If the syndicate does pull out from under me, Espy, I'm ruined. Broke."

Espy fidgeted. *Tell him now,* he said to himself, *before he asks you to do something and you can't refuse him.* But instead, he queried, "What could I do about it?"

"Maybe a lot, Espy. You see, when we bought in with Frank Bowman, we consented to let him go on being the manager. But in event of his death, the syndicate was to be allowed to name the new manager. Frank Bowman is dead. Died of a stroke four weeks ago. Now I'm sending *you* down there as manager."

Espy swallowed hard. He arose unsteadily, then sat down again. He took the cigar from his mouth and noted distractedly that it was dead. "Colonel, I'm just a cattle buyer, not a ranch manager. The boots are too big for me. I can't do it."

The colonel's face puckered. "Espy," he said at length, "you've had it in mind for years to buy a place of your own some day, a place to take your son. If you had a chance to get such a place, you'd grab it in a hurry, wouldn't you? You wouldn't worry about whether or not you could manage it."

Espy's guard came up instinctively. He could feel himself being hazed into a blind trap. "No, sir, I reckon I wouldn't."

"Then, Espy, if you could do it for yourself, you could do it for *me*." The colonel was pointing his cigar like he would point a gun. "There's more to this than just managing a ranch. Much as I hate to admit it, there may be a little something in what Slagel says. That ranch hasn't paid off like it should have. Maybe we've been cheated. Maybe the management is just a little loose.

"I liked Frank Bowman. He seemed like a prince of a man to me. Capable, hard-working, ambitious. And as kind a man as you'd ever run into. But if something's wrong, I want to know about it. And I want it straightened out before Slagel gets there with his wrecking crew."

Espy shook his head. "It's too big for me, Colonel. You ought to send somebody else."

"We have, Espy. The syndicate's had first one man, then another one down there half the time. They weren't of my choosing. Mostly they were just black sheep that some English family wanted to be shed of for a while. All most of them could ever do was get drunk and make obnoxious asses of themselves.

"Geoffrey Spence was the only one of them who was ever worth a dime. He went there about a month before Bowman died. He was smart, that Spence was. Had a way of looking right through you, like he could read everything that was on your mind. He wrote me a couple of letters. There was something down there he didn't like, Espy. He didn't say what it was, but he indicated that he was on the trail of something. Trouble was, he didn't get to finish."

"What happened to him?"

"Well, he was a great hand for hunting. That was his only weakness, I guess. Had a whole set of guns with him. One day he went out to shoot some prairie chickens and didn't come back. They found him dead, shot by his own gun."

"Accident?"

"Looked that way. Must have tripped and shot himself."

Thoughtfully Espy tugged at his ear. "Still, Colonel, if he *had* found something, there's always a chance it wasn't an accident."

Colonel Judkins nodded. "That's why I want you to

go down there. If there's anything wrong, you're the man who can straighten it out. And you're the man who will come back in one piece."

Espy wanted to go. The thought of a return to Texas started needles to prickling his skin, and he could almost taste the sharp, tangy air of the Texas high country, the great, sweeping plains of the Llano Estacada.

But he shook his head. His gaze touched the cabinet where Judkins kept his whisky. "Aren't you forgetting one thing, Colonel?"

Judkins saw what he was looking at. "A year ago, Espy, I wouldn't have dreamed of it. But today, I'd never be afraid of you. Not a bit. I'm willing to bet on you, if you're willing to bet on yourself."

This time it was Espy who walked to the window and stood looking out, his hands clenched. He tasted the gentle drift of dust that came in from over the stockyards, and his mind ran back to other days, and other cattle, and other times he's tasted that dust. There had been a time he would have taken a job like this on the fly, without ever looking back. That was when Jeannie had been alive, and he had been a reckless young cowboy with the world by the tail on a downhill pull.

Lots of things were different now. He wished he had the confidence in himself that the colonel seemed to have in him. That matter of the colonel's whisky. It *had* bothered him, watching the colonel empty that glass. Even after a year or more, it still beckoned him like the legendary mermaids he had read about, luring ships to the rocks. Even now there were times he wrestled with it, wrestled harder than he could admit even to himself.

For there was something a man could do about most of his enemies. He could whip them, kill them, or drive them away. But when his biggest enemy was himself, what was a man to do? He could run and run, yet always his enemy was there, a coyote lurking in the shadows just beyond the campfire, biding its time.

Memory brought the taste of Texas back to him, an early-spring taste, cool and fresh, and sweet with the promise of rain.

But his mind settled on something else, a boy ten years old, a boy who had barely known his father the last three or four years.

"Colonel," Espy said at length, "I hate to turn you down, but you've got to find you somebody else. For a long time now I've had my mind made up. I've promised myself I was going to start staying close to Kenny. I've been on the go a way too much these last few years. Always on the trail, or fixing to leave, or just getting back. But I'm going to change that.

"I'm going to get me a job that'll let me stay here. Something on the stockyards maybe. I'm going to get to know my boy again, the way I used to a long time ago when his mother was living."

There was more he could have said, but that he would have told no man. Like the worrisome reserve that held back the love from Kenny's thin face when Espy went to see him nowadays. It was as if this rough, sun-browned man with the long-reaching look of the plains in his eyes was not his father at all, but, instead, a stranger who occasionally dropped in from some strange land, then rode away again, leaving him as always, in the care of his Aunt Margaret.

There was that night more than a year ago, a memory that always brought an upward surge of shame. Espy Norwood had been in Dodge City, taking delivery on cattle he had bought for the colonel. The hot, dusty day's work over, he had slumped into a chair at a table in the Alhambra and taken his supper from a bottle.

That was his habit often in those days, when the only way he knew to stop memories from tearing at his soul was to keep them drowned in whisky.

Sometime far into the night he had gripped the bottle, shouldered his way through the milling throng that crowded the smoky room, and staggered up the street to the frame hotel. He had been singing some raucous ditty as he weaved up the stairs and shoved open his door, his big hand clenched on the neck of the bottle.

Somehow he got it through his thickened brain that the lamp was burning. Then his cloudy eyes saw them sitting there waiting for him—Jeannie's sister Margaret, and little Kenny. She had brought the boy out from Kansas City for a surprise visit.

Sight of them sobered him the way cold water settles the grounds in a boiling pot of coffee. But it was already too late. As long as he lived, he would never forget the stricken look that chilled the gray eyes of his son.

He had babbled some explanation, but Margaret angrily led the boy out of the room and out of the hotel. In fury at himself, Espy hurled the bottle through the open window. It was the last one he had ever touched.

Espy could see the colonel's shoulders slump in disappointment. "I'm sorry, Colonel," Espy said. "You can find someone better than me. I've got a lot to make up to Kenny for. And I'm going to start now."

III

MARGARET TELLISON owned a fine two-story brick home in a fashionable part of the city. To her views, she had married much better than had her younger sister Jeannie. Her husband was a wealthy merchant who now had three stores in Kansas City and was about to acquire a fourth. The name of Tellison was rapidly rising. It should, for Margaret spent most of her waking hours working toward that end. Who could tell? With the proper social background, Edgar Tellison someday might become a councilman. Even a mayor.

The couple never had had any children. Espy Norwood had often tried to picture Margaret Tellison as a mother. Somehow, the picture never did seem to fit.

But she had offered to give Espy's son a home after Jeannie had died. Bewildered in his loss, Espy had gratefully accepted. And, true to her word, she was bringing him up to be a proper little gentleman. Best private school in Kansas City. Clothes as good as those worn by any rich man's son in town. Manners just as correct as the book could specify.

Wherever they went, Margaret introduced him as "my sister's son." Never a word about the hard-drinking, half-wild Texan who was his father. Kenny Norwood was growing up to be more like Edgar Tellison than like the man whose name he bore.

Espy Norwood stepped down from the horse-drawn cab and handed three jingling coins to the driver. He watched as the cabbie turned his horse around and took the vehicle back down the street in a rolling drift of dust.

Something about the Tellison home always made Espy freeze up inside. Looking at its tall brick walls, its many cupolas, and the two big bay windows that bulged in front, he felt out of place. Times like this, he almost wished Edgar Tellison were a poor man and lived somewhere close to the stockyards. Then maybe Espy could feel at home.

More than that, somehow it took time now to work up the courage to see his son. A cold hand gripped his stomach as he visualized the distrust he would see in Kenny's eyes. It would be there, he knew. It seemed that the gulf which separated them grew wider after every visit, so wide that soon he no longer would be able to bridge it.

"No sense in a grown man being afraid of a little boy," he chided himself. "Just go on in there," Espy held a big box in his hands. He tucked it under his arm and started up the long red brick walk toward the house.

A white-aproned maid answered his nervous knock on the carved front door. Her eyes widened. Espy knew she had to force her smile. "Why, Mr. Norwood. Come in, sir. I'll take you hat."

The hat was brand-new, not even well shaped yet. But she carried it out with her finger tips, as if afraid it would get dirt on her hands.

Espy waited in the parlor, pacing nervously along the wall, looking distractedly at stiff, painted family portraits he had seen twenty times. Officers and gentlemen, probably as farfetched as the horse and bull pictures which the colonel kept on his walls. Espy found that his fingers were shredding the paper in which the box was wrapped, and he set it down.

"Good afternoon, Espy," a woman's voice spoke evenly. He turned.

Margaret Tellison stepped into the parlor, closing a door behind her. She wore a prim, floor-length, black dress with white lace collar. Her back was straight as a diamond-studded walking cane. Her eyes were chilly and without friendliness.

"Hello, Margaret," he spoke politely. "You're looking well."

"Thank you." She motioned toward a chair. "Sit down." She seated herself upon a hard, straight-backed chair, looking like a grim hostess at some painfully formal social affair.

He tried to make some small talk. "Edgar's business is doing well, I guess. See you've done the house over. It looks fine."

She sat with hands in her lap, staring at him, saying no more than was necessary to answer his questions. And he quickly ran out of those.

In facial features, Espy could see her resemblance to Jeannie. The nose was the same. The shape of the chin. The color of the eyes. Margaret Tellison was a pretty woman, in a severe kind of way. Espy had often puzzled over it. How could sisters look so much alike, yet be so completely different?

He had waited as long as he could without asking her. "Where's Kenny? I'm anxious to see him."

She shook her head. "He's not here."

Espy's heart quickened. "Not here? But where is he?"

"We sent him to visit some friends of ours in Chicago. We thought the trip would be broadening for him. He'll be gone another week, or perhaps two."

Espy's breath slowly went out of him. He looked at the floor, an emptiness in him.

Margaret said, "When he returns, I'll tell him you were here."

Espy swallowed his disappointment. "No need. I'll be here to tell him myself."

Alarm began to push into her eyes.

He went on, "I've been away from Kenny too long. I'm going to work in the city from now on, so I can be close to him. It's not right for a boy to grow up a stranger from his own dad."

Incredulous, displeasure evident in her face, she stood up. "Are you serious, Espy?"

"Dead serious."

"Would you take him out of this house?"

He could see what she was driving at. "I'll give him a good home, Margaret, I promise you that. I'll work hard and send him to a good school. And I'll be close, all the time."

Abruptly she turned away from him. She stared out the window, her fingers flexing quickly, angrily. Then she faced him again, her eyes sharp. "I'm going to be blunt, Espy." Her words were chips of ice. "We're giving Kenny a fine opportunity. With us, he has a chance to become someone important, to acquire property and station. What chance has he with you?"

Stung, Espy started to interrupt. She held up her hand impatiently. "No, wait. Hear me out, Espy.

"What could he ever be? A two-bit cowboy, or a down-at-the-heels cattle trader, hanging around the yards? That's not good enough for him, Espy. It may be good enough for you, but not for my sister's son."

Espy strained against the anger that swelled in him. "It won't be that way, Margaret. I have some money saved. I'll give him a good education, and some day we'll have a ranch of our own. All the important people don't live in town."

She started to answer him angrily. But suddenly a voice lifted in another room. It was a boy's voice.

"Aunt Margaret, Aunt Margaret, where are you?"

Espy stiffened. He saw red flush into Margaret Tellison's face.

"I thought you said he was gone."

A door opened, and the boy walked in. "Aunt Margaret, may I—"

He broke off, seeing Espy. He stood there with his mouth open, uncertain as to what to do or say.

Espy warmed at the sight of him. He yearned to draw the youngster to him, to hug him tightly the way he had done when Kenny was a tiny boy, when such a thing wouldn't flush a boy's face with shame.

"Hello, son," Espy said, his voice tight.

"Hello, Daddy."

That's all there was. The warmth in Espy quickly died, and a chill came in its place. He saw in Kenny's eyes the reserve he had dreaded so much. Espy looked down, unsure of himself, cold fear a drag on him. Then he thought of the box.

Forcing a smile, he said, "Say, son, I brought you something."

He handed his son the box and waited tensely while the youngster broke the string and unwrapped the paper. Kenny's eyes lighted up momentarily at the sight of a handsome pair of handmade boots.

Eagerly Espy spoke, "If they don't fit, we can take them back and change them for another pair."

But the light in the boy's eyes died down. He looked at the boots, then at his aunt, his eyes asking if it would be all right to accept the present.

"Take them on up to your room, Kenny," Margaret Tellison said coldly. "Your father and I need to talk."

"Yes, ma'am," the boy said. He left without another glance at Espy. Then he reopened the door. Poking his head in, he said, "Oh, yes, thank you for the boots."

Espy sagged as if a cold, wet blanket had been

thrown across him. "You're welcome, son," he breathed, trying to hold back his disappointment.

Silence stretched taut between Espy and Margaret Tellison. He stared at her, his mouth hardening.

"Well?" she spoke harshly.

"You lied to me, Margaret. You tried to keep me from seeing my boy."

Sharply she replied, "That seems to me the best thing to do. He saw you once before, to his sorrow. That night in Dodge City."

A suspicion had worked in Espy for a long time. Now it struck him again as a dead certainty. "You knew what you would find that night," he said, his voice hardening. "You took Kenny there on purpose."

She squared her shoulders. Anger sent her voice to a higher pitch. "Yes. Yes, I did. It was hard on him. You have no idea how much it hurt him, Espy. But it served its purpose. It drew him away from you, and it made him abandon whatever reserve he had kept up against the kind of life we were trying to give him."

Espy's fists knotted. His eyes were narrowing. "I haven't touched a drop of liquor since that night, Margaret. You know that."

"But you're still Espy Norwood. Because you've been straight for a year doesn't mean you can do it forever. You're the kind that has to quit completely, or not at all. Someday one foot will slip, and nothing will break your fall.

"Besides that, you still live in a world of horses and cattle and sweat and dirt. You live in a world of coarse men and coarse women. I've turned Kenny away from that world, Espy. You won't take him back to it!"

Espy trembled in fury. "He's my son, Margaret, my son. And you've been teaching him to hate me! But that's all over with. I'm taking him with me. Now!"

He started for the door that led out toward the stairs.

Margaret stepped in front of him. "No, Espy, I won't allow it."

Roughly he pushed her aside. He took the steps two at a time and shoved into Kenny's room. "Pack your clothes, Kenny. You're going with me."

Eyes wide, the boy started to protest. In angry impatience Espy threw open the closet door and started ramming clothes into two traveling bags he found there. Kenny watched him, tears brimming in his eyes. Then, resignedly, he began picking up the articles of which he was fondest and putting them into a box.

White-faced, Margaret Tellison stood in the door. "You can't do this, Espy. I'll have the law on you."

"No you won't, Margaret. He's *my* son."

She stood in the doorway, shouting after him as he left. "You won't get away with it, Espy. I'll have him back, you'll see. I'll have him back!"

Two hours later Espy was hammering on Colonel Judkins's door, looking back apprehensively at the forlorn boy who sat in the waiting cab on the street.

A sleepy-eyed colonel opened the door, shoving a lamp out in front of him. "Oh, Espy, it's you. What the devil's gone wrong at this time of night?"

"Nothing wrong, sir. Maybe it's right for the first time. I'll take that Texas job. And Kenny's going with me."

IV

THE FRONTIER town of Mobeetie was taking on some of
the appearances of civilization, although not all the
realities of it. Frame buildings were beginning to rise
among the low-built adobes and picket houses which
huddled along Sweetwater Creek. There was a hotel
now, as good as a man was apt to find way down here
this far from the railroad. There was a livery barn,
operated by the big freighting outfit of Lee & Reynolds.

And it hadn't been long since the citizenry, mostly
buffalo hunters, gamblers, and saloon people, had or-
ganized the county. They'd done a quick job of it,
without the sanction or even the knowledge of most of
the ranchmen who had moved into the territory and set
their huge herds of cattle to grazing the free state-
owned range. As long as law and order was inevitable,
the townspeople wanted to be sure they could adminis-
ter it according to their own lights, and keep it friendly.

Sighting the scattered settlement at the end of the
wagon trail below him, Espy Norwood hauled up on the
reins and stopped the buckboard. He waved his hand
toward the town and glanced at the boy who sat beside
him in silence.

"Mobeetie, son," he said. "We sleep in a real bed
tonight."

The boy nodded wearily. Espy flipped the reins. His
fine team of matched little mules trotted on down old
Charlie Rath's trail that the heavy iron rims of freight
and buffalo-hide wagons had ground to soft powder.
Inwardly, he was at least partly pleased.

From the time they had left Kansas City, a fear had ridden heavy and cold in the bottom of his stomach. But there hadn't been a whimper out of Kenny, not one. Kenny's thin face, normally tending to paleness, was blistered a fiery red by the hot sun and the constant wind which never halted in its restless search across the broad reaches of the Llano Estacado. The boy's gray eyes were dulled with weariness. The man and the boy had been polishing the hard, flat seat of the buckboard from sunup to dark every day since they had stepped down off the train at Dodge and turned their faces south.

It had been a long, monotonous, almost endless trip down across the plains, where the horizon was the same, hour after hour, almost as if a man had been standing still.

"It's a mighty big land," somebody had said once, speaking of the great Staked Plains. "It just goes on and on and on, without ever an end to it. It's like looking into Eternity itself."

There hadn't been a word of complaint from Kenny.

But there had been few words of any kind, and that was bothering Espy as he watched the youngster's tired eyes taking in the raw town ahead. He sensed the boy's immediate disappointment.

"Not much like Kansas City, son," he admitted. "But you'll like this country, once you get used to it."

Kenny said nothing. His thin lips had been tight and silent since the day Espy had stormed into his room and hauled him out of Aunt Margaret's house.

Espy thought of Colonel Judkins—how tickled the old man had been when Espy told him he would come to Texas after all, and bring Kenny with him.

"Give that boy a month of fresh air and Texas sunshine," Judkins had smiled, "and he'll never want to see the city again."

His short beard spread wide by a grin, the colonel had then admitted, "You don't know how worried I was for a while today, Espy. I was so sure you'd go, I wrote a letter to Frank Bowman's daughter a week ago. Told her you'd be there to take over the managership."

Espy Norwood hauled up the buckboard in front of Huselby's hotel. Stiffly he stepped down, wrapping the reins around the front wheel. He reached up to help Kenny. But the boy climbed down on the off side, alone.

Espy stood there scanning the irregular rows of indifferent buildings, some of them frame but most of them rude adobe or picket shacks. The sun was a flaming red, low in the west, like a candle flickering bright just before going out. This was an awkward hour for the town, caught in the transition between the business activity of the day and the boisterous playtime of night.

Down toward the end of the street he sighted a settler with a wagonload of buffalo bones. Not a great many settlers here yet, he knew. But there were enough to set the pattern. It wouldn't be many years before they would control a big part of this country, and the free range days would be gone. The man who didn't own his land or have a lease on it would find himself shoved out.

Down the powdery street Espy's eye caught the name painted on a sign above a long, narrow frame building. "Buffalo Bar. Best Bourbon in Texas. Arch McCavitt, Prop."

The name brightened Espy's leathery, stubbled face with the pleasure of remembered days, a time long ago when there hadn't been any trouble in the world, and everything worth having was free.

Espy turned back to the buckboard. He gripped Kenny's suitcase and flung his own warbag over his shoulder.

"Come on, son," he said, walking up to the big front door of the hotel. "Let's go see about that bed."

The hotel had a bathtub, and Espy used it. He sharpened his long straight razor and shaved off the rough whiskers that had grown on the trail down from Dodge. Watching Kenny splashing in the tub, washing himself with the rough slab of poor soap, Espy remembered how much of a fight he had used to put up when he was a kid, any time Ma brought up the subject of a bath. But Kenny had been eager to wash the trail dust off. Kansas City training, Espy thought. Bath twice a week, and oftener if necessary. That didn't hurt a boy any. But baths were likely to come more seldom out here.

They started to the dining room together. Espy placed his big hand on his son's shoulder, then ruefully removed it when he felt the boy begin to pull away.

A heavy-set, middle-aged woman came out of the kitchen to wait on them, her long skirt sweeping the floor behind her.

Espy said, "This boy here's been doing on canned tomatoes and sardines and stuff like that all the way down from Dodge. I want you to fill him up on some good Texas beef tonight, ma'am."

He felt a quick pleasure at the shy smile which flickered on the boy's face. The first he had seen.

While they waited, two more customers came in. They were young women, and Espy knew at a glance that they weren't of the kind most numerous in towns like this. He immediately placed them as women in from a ranch.

One of them, wearing a wedding band, he judged to be a little younger than himself. She wasn't pretty. Some men might even call her plain. But her face bore a compelling friendliness, and permanent laugh wrinkles had settled comfortably at the corners of her eyes.

Espy knew the cowboys. He was certain that wher-

ever she lived, cowboys probably would ride miles out
of their way to happen by the house at mealtime. It was
an unquestioned custom out here that drifting
cowhands be fed. He knew by instinct that she would be
one who would feed them cheerfully. In return they
would fetch water for her, and see that the woodbox
behind the stove was as full as it would go. And maybe
they would whittle out a toy gun or a doll for her kids, if
she had any. To see a good woman once in a while, to
hear the lilt of her pleasant talk, filled a need for
cowboys on the woman-shy plains that no number of
trips to a ribald town could ever do.

Espy's gaze turned to the other woman. She was a
few years younger, in her mid-twenties, he guessed.
His interest rose. Here *was* a pretty one. He liked the
mature features on her soft-skinned face. Her nose
tilted upward at the end, a saucy tilt that suggested good
humor. But the lamplight picked up a glint of red from
her smooth-brushed auburn hair, and her blue eyes
looked as if they could snap like a whip when the
occasion called for it.

The blue eyes lifted to his face, and he quickly
dropped his gaze, feeling the color rise under his skin.
A man could stare all he wanted to at the girls in a dance
hall. But here it was different.

He remembered how it had been with Jeannie, the
first time he had met her. His mind drifted back in
pleasant memory while his gaze fastened on the frayed
edge of the tablecloth. The lamplight seemed to close in
around him. He remembered himself and Arch
McCavitt, wild young cowboys still on the sunny side
of their twenties, headed for town in high good humor
to see the elephant and buck the tiger. Two months' pay
was burning in their pockets, and a dozen dance-hall
girls were waiting to help them put out the fire.

Riding into town, they had spurred their horses into a hard lope and commenced shooting the sky full of holes to serve notice on all and sundry that the team of Norwood & McCavitt had arrived. Ahead of them two girls were riding in a buggy. Their horses misunderstood the cowboys' intentions and headed for the high country as fast as the buggy could bounce.

It was Espy who managed to catch up with them and pull the runaways to a reluctant halt. He took a tight grip on the buggy reins and spoke softly to the boogered, eye-rolling team. In the buggy seat, one girl was shaking her fist and speaking none too softly to Espy and to the late-arriving Arch McCavitt. That was Margaret.

But as shame flooded hot into Espy's face, he had looked at the other girl, and caught the spark of laughter in her eyes. She winked while her sister rattled on and on. This was Jeannie.

Now a thin smile came to Espy's face as he remembered. It had been a long time. It had taken years to do, but finally, through a stern will, he had put the grief and loss behind him. Now he could remember with pleasure, and without regret.

The clatter of a heavy plate jarred him out of his reverie. The plump woman set down two thick panfried steaks in front of him and Kenny. She brought a chipped platter full of fried potatoes and a plate of hot biscuits, followed by a cup of coffee for Espy. In a moment she set down a pitcher of milk for the boy, and Espy wondered idly where she got it. Not many milk cows in this country. Not many people would've drunk milk even if they'd had the chance.

A desperate trail-born hunger temporarily robbed Kenny of his reserve. Discarding the gentle manners his Aunt Margaret had drilled into him, he dug into the steak like a half-starved puppy tearing at a caught rabbit. Espy watched him with a lingering smile of pleasure.

Two men came into the dining room together. Espy first noticed the quick frown of displeasure in the face of the plump old woman. He glanced across his shoulder.

Both men bore a rough, back-trail look, with a careless growth of whiskers you couldn't rightly call a beard. The shortest of the two weaved slightly as he walked. His hip pocket bulged. Although his pulled-out shirttail covered most of it, it was obvious what caused the bulge. Seeing the women, he pulled off his shapeless hat. Beneath it a mop of rusty-colored hair sprang up like a careless growth of weeds, with strands of silver shining in the lamplight.

The other man was taller, with shoulders as broad across as the length of a shotgun barrel. His dirty blue shirt, buttoned to the collar, fit snugly across a powerful chest. His eyes touched Espy, eyes black as the thick stubble of barbed-wire whiskers bristling on his big chin. They were beliggerent eyes, the kind that were perpetually looking for a fight.

The shorter man stumbled against a table, caught himself, then weaved up beside the table where the two women sat. "Good evening, Mary," he said thickly to the younger woman.

She studiously ignored him, a splotch of angry color in her cheeks. The man stared at her, turning sullen. He had the florid face and swimmy eyes of the habitual drunkard.

"You getting too good to speak to your kinfolks anymore?"

She gave him a quick, raking glance. "You don't belong in here. You're drunk, and you're making a fool of yourself. Now get out."

His blood-laced eyes stared at the girl while his lips trembled with angry words unsaid. After a moment he turned and tromped out, walking into a chair and knocking it over, and sending another one clattering back in precarious balance against a table. The broad-shouldered, black-whiskered man followed him, his dark face unmoved.

The young woman buried her anger in the eating of her meal, while the other one sat in silent understanding.

Kenny had watched the scene with wide eyes. Now it was forgotten again, as far as he was concerned, and he hungrily dug into his steak. That done, he got around a big slab of pie which the elderly woman had brought.

Espy sensed that the two women were watching the boy, too. The younger one's eyes met Espy's, and he saw the gentle amusement that had come into them, displacing her anger. He warmed to her, wondering why. The answer hit him suddenly and hard. Those were the same eyes Jeannie used to have.

The young woman picked up her piece of pie and brought it over to Espy's table. "Somehow I'm not very hungry tonight," she smiled. "Maybe this young man would like to eat my pie."

Kenny's eyes lighted up. He looked to Espy for permission.

"Thank the lady, son," Espy said.

Kenny did, and piled into the pie.

Supper finished, Espy could see that some of the weariness had drained from the kid's blistered face. More contentment showed there now than at any time since they had left Kansas City.

"You're doing fine, son," Espy thought. "And someday maybe you'll even like me again."

As the dark blanket of twilight settled over the prairie town, a new and vibrant life began to surge down its crooked, dusty course. Horses plodded up and down the street. Spurs jingled, and boots clumped heavily on what plank porches there were. High-spirited talk rose with the moon, and somewhere off yonder a fiddle began to saw away.

Espy stayed in the room until Kenny crawled into the hard bed and dropped off to sleep. He pulled the blanket up over the boy. His eyes were soft as he watched a long moment the gentle rise and fall of the boy's breathing. Then he stepped back to the door, trimmed the lamp, and blew out the flame.

Outside, he stood a moment in front of the hotel, watching the lively foot and horse traffic up and down the street. He stepped into the sand and angled across to the place where he had seen the sign.

The Buffalo Bar was a long, narrow building with a pine bar running along one wall, up toward the front. Down the other wall was a careless scattering of card tables. In back were closed doors leading, Espy figured, to small private rooms. These could be used for big-stake games where the players didn't want a crowd hanging around, watching over their shoulders. Or they could be used for other purposes, too. But, looking around, Espy saw no girls.

A loud cowboy whoop ripped loose down at the far end of the room. Arch McCavitt came striding toward him, hand outstretched, his face glowing. "Espy Norwood! I wouldn't even have thought of you for a five-dollar gold piece!"

Espy pumped McCavitt's hand, enjoying the sight of that happy-go-lucky face. He bent forward for a close look at McCavitt's flaming red hair.

"Not a streak of gray in it, Arch. The years've been kind to you."

McCavitt laughed, "Aw, I just rinse it now and

again with that stuff the girls use down at Kansas Kate's place."

He slapped Espy's shoulder and led him back toward a table at the far end. He made a quick signal to the bartender. "Lord, Espy, it's sure good to see you. Been a lot of years, a lot of years. Where've you been? How's Jeannie?"

Espy's face pinched. "Jeannie's dead, Arch. Been dead for five years."

Arch McCavitt's grip tightened on Espy's shoulder. Espy quickly changed the subject. "Well, Arch, looks like the only thing different about you is that you're a little older. You haven't changed a bit."

The bartender brought a bottle and two glasses. Arch started to fill them. Espy reached out and covered one of the glasses with his big hand. "None for me, Arch. I'm not using it anymore."

McCavitt looked quizzically at him. "Man, *you've* sure changed." To the bartender, McCavitt called, "Jud, come back here and get this stuff. You know I don't ever drink this early."

The two sat back, silent a while, enjoying each other's company the way old friends will. Arch rolled a cigarette with one hand, like he used to do as a young hell-for-leather cowboy, to show off. He had done it so long that it was second nature with him now. Espy was sure a lot of the old recklessness still clung to him. It showed in his face, his eyes, and the bright, clean cut of the fancy clothes he wore. It wouldn't all be burned out of him if he lived to be ninety.

Espy said, "I never would've thought about running into you here, Arch. But it looks like you've found you a good spot."

Arch's gaze swept the raw frame saloon, a warm pride glowing in his face. "Not the ritziest joint in the country, and I don't keep girls here like some of them do. But I still have a lot of business, Espy. Drinks and games. I try to keep an honest place. Man comes here, he knows he's not fixing to get cheated.''

Curiosity burned in Arch McCavitt's dancing blue eyes. ''What brings *you* down here, anyway? Last I heard, you were up in Wyoming, working for Colonel Judkins.''

Espy nodded. ''I'm still working for him, Arch. Going to manage the Figure 4 outfit for him and for the syndicate.''

McCavitt suddenly frowned, his fingers pinching the cigarette so hard that it went out.

Espy saw it. ''What's the matter, Arch? Maybe you can tell me what I'm getting into.''

McCavitt dropped the cigarette into an empty sardine can that served as an ash tray. ''Getting into? I wouldn't say that you're getting into anything in particular. The Figure 4's pretty much the same as the rest of the ranches around here. Bigger than most. Better cow country.''

Espy sensed something evasive in Arch's answer. ''Arch, the colonel and some of the stockholders seem to have an idea there's something wrong out there. You know this country. What do you think?''

Arch studied the tabletop, his face puckering. ''I wouldn't say there's anything wrong. A little cow stealing along, of course. They'll always steal from an English outfit. You can't stop them.''

''I can stop them. There's a law.''

A touch of humor flickered in McCavitt's eyes. ''Espy, you can read your lawbooks from Apple to Zebra, and you won't find any law there against stealing cows from an Englishman.''

Espy pointed out, ''Frank Bowman was half owner,

and his daughter still is. They're just as American as a Rebel yell."

He waited for an answer to that and got none. He leaned forward, studying McCavitt's face. "Tell me about Frank Bowman. Was he honest?"

McCavitt said, "I've never known a man I liked any better. Heart as big as a barn door. Ride from one end of the Panhandle to the other and you'll never find a man who'll say a word against him."

Espy eased back into his chair, chewing his lip. Maybe the colonel's suspicions were wrong. Lots of things could account for a ranch not making the money it ought to even with a good manager. Cattle thieves, storms, dry spells. Sometimes the very size of an outfit made it hard to operate efficiently. On a big, unwieldly spread, often it was impossible to keep the right hand posted as to what the left hand was doing.

"What do you think of his daughter, Arch?"

McCavitt smiled, his eyes softening. "Mary? She's . . . she's . . . Well, the only time I ever wish I was something besides a saloonman is when I see her." He pointed his finger at Espy. "Don't you ever do anything to hurt Mary. If you do, you'll have me to whip."

He said it good-naturedly. But Espy knew he meant it. "Look, Arch," he said with a smile. "I'm not here to try to make anybody out a thief. I'm just here to see if we can get the outfit to making a little more money. Got to keep the Bank of England strong, you know."

A girl stepped out of one of the rooms in the back of McCavitt's saloon, closing the door behind her. She looked around, spotted McCavitt, and came walking toward him, smiling. She wore a gray silk dress, cut low at the neck and clinging tightly to an amply-round figure. Espy had no trouble in classifying her, although he knew that she fitted in somewhere near the top of her class.

Arch stood up quickly, catching her hand and leading her to the table. "Lilybelle," he said grinning, "I want you to meet an old *compadre* of mine, Espy Norwood. We used to cowboy together, way back when the Guadalupe Mountains were just holes in the ground. Espy, this is Lilybelle."

No sir, Espy thought, Arch hadn't changed a bit. But his taste wasn't bad. Lilybelle was strikingly pretty. And her blue eyes were bright and intelligent, not empty and dumb as in so many such girls.

"I have to come in and check up on Arch occasionally," she said, her fingers running gently through Arch's reddish hair. Real affection softened her voice. "His arithmetic never was much good. He forgets to count his drinks sometimes."

Arch shrugged. "Lilybelle watches after me. She henpecks me like an old wife."

And Espy could tell that Arch liked it.

When Lilybelle had returned to the back room, Espy chuckled. "Thought you said there weren't any girls in here."

Arch flushed, still grinning. "There aren't. Not for the general public, anyway. That's strictly the property of the house."

As Espy started to leave, Arch took his hand. "You be carefully, cowboy. I remember the last syndicate man who went out there. He's dead."

"But that was an accident—wasn't it?"

Arch frowned, then nodded. "Yeah. Yeah, I guess it was. But just the same, you be careful."

A deep worry dragged heavily at Espy as he walked out into the sandy street and started back afoot toward the lantern-lit hotel. Arch had been cautious about it, but he had made it plain—Espy had better watch his step. So there *was* something wrong, somewhere.

In his room, Espy struck a match on the sole of his boot and relighted the lamp, his face twisting to the sharp bite of burning sulphur in his nostrils. He straightened suddenly, in alarm. Kenny's bed was empty.

At a glance Espy saw that the boy's clothes were gone from where he had draped them across the straight back of a rawhide-bottomed chair. He swung out into the hall, his heartbeat quickening.

Down the short hall he saw the yellow flicker of lamplight through an open doorway. Maybe somebody there had seen the kid. Espy strode hurriedly to the door, then stopped abruptly. There Kenny sat, comfortable in a high-backed rocking chair. Talking pleasantly to him were the two young women Espy had seen in the dining room.

The older of the two saw Espy first. Arising, she smiled warmly. Somehow, she didn't look so plain now as she had at first. There was a fetching comeliness to her face. "Come in, Mr. Norwood. We've been trying to make friends with your son."

Relief eased through Espy. He relaxed, returning her smile. "What happened, Kenny?"

The boy hesitated in answering him. The woman said, "Some cowboys were racing their horses down the street while ago, hollering and raising cain. The noise woke the boy up. He found himself in the dark, in a strange room. Naturally he was scared.

"We saw him come out into the hall, and we invited him to come in and talk with us till his father got back."

Espy smiled. "You get much conversation out of him?"

The younger woman answered that. "Not much. He's pretty shy. About all we found out was that you all are on your way to the Figure 4."

Her blue eyes studied him with interest. "Are you a cattle buyer?"

Espy stood there awkwardly, his hat heavy in his hands. "Well, yes and no. That's my usual business. But I'm not down here to buy cattle this time."

The girl made a mock frown. "Oh? That's too bad. We always welcome a cattle buyer out at the Figure 4."

The surprise showed in his face. Apologetically she said. "I'm sorry, I forgot to tell you who we are. Mr. Norwood, this is Helen Kirk." She swung her slender hand back toward the older woman, the one with the easy, warming smile. Espy bowed, bending slightly forward from the waist with the inborn chivalry of the old-time cowboy.

"Helen's husband is Sam Kirk, foreman of the Figure 4 for a good many years now," the girl said.

Espy waited for the girl's name, but he guessed it even before she spoke again.

"I'm Mary Bowman. Frank Bowman was my father."

Espy studied her a moment. "Then you're the one I want to see, I guess. Colonel Judkins sent me."

"The colonel?" Her eyes widened. "You're not English. I had begun to believe the syndicate employed nothing but Englishmen."

Espy told her, "They slipped this time. I've never been east of Kansas City."

Solemnly she said, "I'm sorry the colonel didn't send me word, but I can guess why he sent you. And I think you can take a good report back to him.

"I'll be a good manager, Mr. Norwood. I worked with Dad enough to know pretty well how he ran things. The colonel will have nothing to worry about.''

Suddenly uneasy, Espy asked. ''Didn't you get a letter from the colonel, about me?''

She shook her head.

She doesn't know why I'm here, he thought bleakly. And he knew suddenly that she would take it hard when she *did* find out.

In her blue eyes he saw a silent strength, a driving determination. He knew instinctively that she had stepped into her father's boots with firm resolution. Having someone wrest the managership from her now, without warning, would hit her like the strike of a club. Somehow, Espy knew she wouldn't break easily. She probably wouldn't break at all. She'd fight.

Just as well tell her now, he argued with himself. He had the words, but he couldn't say them. Tomorrow, maybe. Or later, at the ranch. He'd wait until the time was right. For he found himself liking this girl, liking the solid strength he saw in her. Maybe he could find a way that wouldn't hurt so much.

Walking with Kenny back to their room, Espy passed a man in the nearly-dark hallway. Wobbly on his feet, the man stopped, propping himself against the wall to stare at Espy. His heavy breath reached far out ahead of him. Espy recognized him as the man who had come weaving into the dining room earlier. Espy gave him a cold passing glance, then turned in through the open door, Kenny following closely behind him.

When Espy's door closed, the whiskered man staggered on down the hall. He stopped and pounded on the women's door. Mary Bowman opened it cautiously. Seeing him, she let the door swing open. Her eyes brittle, she placed her hands on her slim hips. ''All right, Uncle Gid, what do you want? Money?''

He blustered with a thick tongue. ''Do you think I'm one to go begging off of my kinfolks?''

Her answer was crisp. "Yes! You sponged off of Dad for years. How much do you want?"

He shook his head, muttering something under his breath. "I ain't looking for money. I just wanted to know something. That man who left here—was his name Norwood?"

"Yes, Espy Norwood. The colonel sent him."

"Did he tell you why?"

A worried tone edged into her voice. "Not exactly. I guess he's here to see how things are going since Dad died."

Gid Bowman shook his shaggy head, looking down the hall toward Norwood's door. "I didn't figure he'd tell you right off. He's come to take the place away from you. He didn't tell you that, did he, Mary?"

She grabbed him by the shoulders and shook him sharply. "What are you talking about?"

"He's here to take over the ranch. He's going to be the manager now. *Him*, Mary, not you. You're out. For ten years that ranch was yours and your dad's. Now he's going to shove you out.

"The syndicate's been trying to do it ever since they bought in. Your dad finally saw that. You better wake up too, Mary. Wake up before you find yourself without that ranch."

Her lips drew thin. Color flooded her cheeks. "You're lying."

He shook his head. "Ask *him*. Ask him if I'm lying."

She stood uncertainly in the doorway, her fists clenched. Then determinedly she shoved past the half-drunken man and strode angrily down the hall. She pounded on Espy Norwood's door.

Espy saw at a glance the way her blue eyes were crackling. It took him by surprise.

"Are you sure you told me all of it, Mr. Norwood?"

"All of it? I'm afraid I don't savvy, ma'am."

Her finger pointed straight at him, like a bayonet. "Did the colonel send you here to take the management away from me?"

Uncomfortably Espy tried to feel out his ground like a horse in deep mud. "It's not exactly that way, Miss Bowman. He didn't know you'd figured on being the manager yourself. He figured . . ."

She cut him off, her voice sharp as barbed wire. "He figured that with Dad gone he could run this place to suit himself—that it wouldn't be hard to take it away from a woman. But he'll find out differently, Norwood, I promise you that."

Her eyes blazed. "This is one woman who knows what belongs to her. And she knows how to keep it. You'd better go back where you came from, mister. You've never seen trouble like the trouble you'll run into if you try to take my ranch away from me!"

And while Espy stood there open-mouthed, trying to think of an answer, she turned and strode back down the hall.

V

Espy headed the mules southeastward, down a wagon road the livery stable hostler had pointed out to him. The road was a plain one, well-carved in the prairie sod by the wide iron tires of freight wagons that had found the shortest, yet the easiest, route for their teams of mules and oxen.

The morning carried them across a gentle, rolling country which fell back toward the broken ground and the brushy draws of the cap rock. Far as a man could see, there was little or no timber to break the easy swell and fall of the great domain of grass. It was cow country. Spring rains had brought the short grass up to boot-top level and more. The flag tops bent downward in reverence to the ever-searching wind, the ceaseless wind working southward from an endless sweep of open prairie that stretched most of the way to Canada.

By a wagon-seat guess, Espy figured they were about halfway to the Figure 4 headquarters by the time he reached into a box and brought out the cold lunch he had fixed up in the hotel dining room.

Kenny wolfed cold steak and cold biscuits. Watching him, Espy smiled. There was a heap of satisfaction in watching a hungry boy eat. Made a man remember how good some things had tasted to him once. Made him wish the maturity of years hadn't robbed him of the simple pleasure which a boy could get out of a meal, be it hot, cold, or indifferent.

"Twenty-five or thirty miles out, the trail skirts by

the west side of a big lake," the hostler had said. "It forks two ways there. You just take the right-hand fork and keep bearing south. You'll get there bye and bye."

Espy found the lake, or rather the lake bed. Weeds stood green and rank, and the grass was far taller than on the sloping land that shed its water into the sprawling natural basin. There was no water in it now, however. Spring rains had been good, that much was apparent. But there had been no rain in the last couple of months. The prairie grass had begun to burn a light brown under the summer sun, and the team's hoofs stirred up a nose-pinching smell of dry dust.

The right-hand fork led on into rougher country, where the green foliage of scattered mesquite and cedar brush broke into the even brown of the curing grass.

The mules sensed the horsemen before Espy saw them. The animals poked their long ears forward and lifted their heads in sudden interest. Just ahead, the wagon road skirted the edge of a mesquite thicket, which followed down a long draw toward another dry lake. Four horsemen moved out from the thicket and reined up in the trail, a hundred yards ahead.

One of the men swung down easily and dropped the reins. He leaned his shoulder lazily against the saddle and waited there, watching Espy's buckboard. He was a big man, six feet tall, and maybe an inch or so more. He was broad-shouldered and black-bearded, and instantly Espy remembered him. This man had walked into the dining room last night with the florid-faced drunk.

The man's eyes challenged Espy. They were eyes black as the thick mat of whiskers on his square jaw. Espy reined up almost abreast of him. The man took a step forward. The black eyes raked Espy, shifted a second to the boy, then lifted to Espy's face again. His voice was almost a growl.

"You're another Englishman on your way to the Figure 4, ain't you?"

A quick resentment moved in Espy. "I'm on my way to the Figure 4."

The black-bearded man scowled. "We got no place for foreigners here. This country is for Americans. So turn that rig around and head it back to where you came from."

Anger smoldered in Espy, waiting for one quick breath to explode it into flame. "I've come a long way to get here. I don't intend to quit now."

The big man rocked back on his high heels, the beginnings of a hard grin breaking across his broad mouth, his knotty fists lifting. "Been hoping you'd say that," he spoke. "I been looking forward to thrashing me an Englishman. Git down from that rig."

Espy made no move. The three horsemen drew guns. The big man jerked his head sideways, motioning toward them. "They mean business. No telling what might happen if guns was to go to popping. Might even hurt that boy there. You better climb down, like I told you."

Boxed. There was no way out of this, Espy knew. And the big man outweighed him by forty pounds.

Kenny spoke out in a frightened, high-pitched voice. "Daddy, tell him you're not . . ."

"Hush, son."

Climbing down, Espy wondered how the big man had known of his coming.

He stood little chance, he knew, unless his lighter weight might make him quicker on his feet. And unless he could use surprise. . . .

As his foot touched the ground, Espy's hand reached behind the buckboard seat. His fingers closed upon the handle of a traveling bag. With all the strength in him he hurled the bag right into the big man's face.

He sprang in behind it, driving a hard right fist straight into the rider's eye. In the two seconds that the man staggered back, Espy drove one blow into his prickly jaw and another into his stomach.

His opponent cried out in rage and surged at him, his fists swinging like a pair of sledges. This was a bulldog kind of fighter. He would use his weight and his mighty strength to win. He could afford to swap blows because his own would be the hardest.

Espy managed to dodge the first swinging fists and crowd in. He landed some hard licks to the big face which was reddened with blistering rage. But he didn't expect that luck to hold. The big fists began to rock him. Pain ripped him. Half the breath was jarred out of him. It was as if a big bull had pinned him against a fence and was slamming its huge head into him. Espy's fists weren't hitting so hard now.

But the other man was slower, too. His lips were broken, and blood explored the heavy black whiskers. One eye was swelling shut.

Then, suddenly, Espy got his chance. The big man missed him with a broad swing of his fist, and the dark face was wide open for a hard wallop. Espy swung. He felt a savage exultation as his fist drove into the other eye.

The big rider squalled out and doubled over against the slashing pain. Breathing hard, Espy pressed what advantage he had won, driving the man back, and back again, until he fell against the buckboard. The mules, badly boogered, jumped in the traces and rocked the rig. Then Espy had a new worry, that they would run away, dragging the helpless boy with them.

Blindly the big man rushed Espy. Espy stepped aside far enough to take nothing worse than a glancing lick. Almost exhausted, he swayed back in then and started slashing his tired fists mercilessly into the big man's face and stomach. He realized he had won. There was grim satisfaction in the knowledge. But he knew they wouldn't leave him alone. One of the other riders would take up the fight, and Espy couldn't last. He was almost ready to cave in now.

He saw one rider step down from the saddle, and he swayed around to face him. But he was powerless to help himself. He saw the gun barrel lift and arc toward his head, and he couldn't dodge it. Pain exploded in him. He dropped to his hands and knees and tried to stop himself there. But the gun struck him again, and he toppled forward into a black hole that had no bottom.

The rider holstered his gun and looked at Espy Norwood, sprawled limply in the dry grass.

"Got a head as hard as a rock," he muttered, half in admiration. "That's the fightingest Englishman ever I saw."

The black-bearded man was still down on one knee, rubbing his bruised and battered face and leaving angry smears of red. His coarse hair was tousled like the shaggy coat of a big black dog. He was talking to himself under his breath.

The smaller rider caught him under the arms and helped him sway to his feet. "Git up, Quirt. The fight's over, and you'd just as well run up the Union Jack. The Englishman whipped you."

Kenny Norwood had sat on the buckboard seat in ashen-faced silence. Now an old loyalty came rushing back to him, mixed with a flood of anger.

"He's *not* an Englishman," he bawled. "He's from Texas. And he'll whip all of you, you just wait and see!"

"Shut up!" the big man scowled. Cursing, he kicked Espy Norwood in the ribs.

"By God, he'll wish he'd never even heard of the Figure 4," he exploded. "You, Jake, unhitch them mules. Mose, you and Pete throw down that stuff from the buckboard. Scatter it from hell to breakfast.''

Kenny jumped down and knelt beside his father. His widened eyes watched in terror while the men wreaked havoc with the clothes, the bedding, the saddles and gear on the buckboard.

Finally satisfied, the four men climbed back upon their horses. The big man had to have help. His eyes swollen almost shut, he reined in close to the boy. ''Listen now, kid. When your old man wakes up, tell him this is only a sample. We're taking the mules. Maybe the long walk back to Mobeetie will give him time to do a little thinking. Tell him he better not come back. Next time, they'll have to carry him away in a box.''

The four men wheeled their horses around and disappeared into the thicket, driving the two mules before them. Kenny listened until the hoofbeats faded away to the southwest. Then he got up and hunted for the water jug. He found it on the ground. Luckily, they hadn't broken it. He took a handkerchief from his pocket, poured water on it, and started wiping his father's face, fighting the panic that throbbed in his quick heartbeat and held a tight grip on his small throat.

''Daddy,'' he pleaded, ''Daddy, wake up.''

Full consciousness was slow in coming back to Espy. Nausea came with it. He clasped his hands over his stomach, where pain cut like the sharp swipe of a bowie knife. He turned away from Kenny and let the sickness come up out of him. The nausea ebbed then, but the pain throbbed on, numbing pain that beat at every part of him.

He took the wet handkerchief from his son's hand. Kenny knelt in front of him, dumb with shock, his eyes sick as they stared at his father's raw, bruised face.

''It's all right, son,'' Espy said in a low, tight voice.

"It's over with now. Everything's going to be all right."

Kenny blurted it out in a voice shrill with excitement. "They took our mules, Daddy. They scattered out everything we had. They said if we ever came back they'd kill you."

With Kenny's help, Espy swayed to his feet. He leaned heavily against the buckboard, waiting for strength. It was slow in returning.

"Made a right smart of a mess, didn't they?" he said, forcing a grin for the boy's benefit. It hurt, and he let it go. "We better get started cleaning it up."

Espy made an effort, but it was no use. He sat on the ground, leaning back against a buckboard wheel, his arms folded tightly across his middle. He watched while Kenny gathered up their belongings, scattered out over two acres of grass. Grunting, the boy lifted Espy's saddle up into the buckboard. Then he picked up his own, a boy's-size saddle which still smelled strongly of new leather. Espy had bought it for him in Dodge City. He had wondered at the time if Kenny would ever use it. The boy had shown no such inclination.

Kenny began picking up their clothes and shoving them back into the traveling bags. He held up one of Espy's shirts, which had been ripped in two.

"Might as well throw it away, son," Espy said, shaking his head. "And anything else that's torn up that bad."

A good part of the clothing was. Mentally Espy marked it off as a loss. Not a bad one, though. Aside from the beating, it was the loss of the little mules which bothered him most. They had cost a hundred dollars in Dodge. Man didn't find a team like that just anywhere.

When their gear had been placed back in the

buckboard, Kenny asked worriedly, "What are we going to do now?"

"We might wait here a week and not see anybody, son. We just as well start walking."

"Back to town?"

Espy shook his head. "We're about as close to the Figure 4 as we are to town. We'll go that way."

Fear looked out of Kenny's eyes. "But, Daddy, they said—" He swallowed the rest of it in resignation.

Espy slung a canteen over his shoulder, dropped a little food into a sack, and started walking. Kenny was close behind him.

By the time he had gone a hundred yards, Espy knew it was no use. He let the canteen slip from his shoulder, then eased himself to the ground, breathing hard.

"It's no go, son. I couldn't walk from here to that rise yonder." He grinned crookedly. "Looks like another dry camp for us tonight."

Aching, Espy stretched out in the shade under the buckboard to rest. Tomorrow he might be able to make it. Not today.

He had lain there perhaps half an hour when Kenny looked up, then jumped to his feet. The boy pointed back down the Mobeetie trail. "Somebody's coming."

Espy sat up and looked. A buckboard. He squinted, trying to see better. But his eyes were bruised and watery.

Kenny said, "It's the two ladies, Daddy."

Mary Bowman was driving. She reined her buckboard to a halt. She took in the whole scene in one glance. Her eyes were wide for just a moment. Then they hardened.

"What happened?"

Espy said, "Reception committee."

Mrs. Kirk's face was white. Her eyes softened in

quick sympathy. Instantly she climbed down, looking apprehensively at the boy.

"Are you all right, son?"

Kenny nodded. "But they hurt Daddy."

The kindly woman turned her sympathetic gaze toward Espy. "How bad? Any bones broken?"

He shook his head. "No. There's nothing that won't heal."

She looked at Espy's face, gently searching over it with her fingers. "Couple of bad cuts there," she said softly. "We'll fix those soon as we get to the ranch."

Espy said pointedly, "Miss Bowman hasn't said she was going to take us."

He glanced up at the girl. She gave him a rocky look, one that set him to wondering.

"We'll take you," said the girl. "If it was just you, I'd leave you. But we can't leave that boy. Throw your things on the back. One of the cowboys will come tomorrow and get the rig."

Kenny transferred their belongings. There was barely room for them all because the women were bringing several packages from town, along with a couple of traveling bags.

Mrs. Kirk asked wonderingly, "Now, why would anybody want to do a thing like this to you?"

"They talked like they figured I was an Englishman, and they just don't like Englishmen." Espy watched Mary Bowman's face for a reaction. He saw none. He hadn't been fooled by that business about being English. He knew that was just an excuse. Briefly he described the men.

Helen Kirk mused. "Big man, black eyes, black beard. A good many men around here could fit a description like that."

Kenny spoke up. "One of them called him Quirt."

Helen Kirk glanced quickly at Mary Bowman.

Something flickered in the girl's blue eyes, then covered up again.

"Quirt Wolford," Mrs. Kirk said. "There are a good many tough men around here, but there's a difference between tough and bad. Quirt Wolford's bad."

Kenny squeezed onto the seat beside the women. Espy hunched in the back, his legs hanging over. The bouncing over the rough spots in the trail doubled the ache that throbbed through him.

Presently Mary Bowman looked back at him. "You must be a tough man yourself, Norwood."

"Why?"

"If you hadn't been, you'd have turned back after what happened to you. Didn't you want to?"

Espy narrowed his eyes, studying her. "No. If anything, it just settled a few doubts."

She looked away from him, to the trail ahead of her. He stared at the back of the wide, flowered bonnet she wore. He wondered, and the wonder changed to a half-angry certainty. Someone had sicked Quirt Wolford onto him. Who else could it have been?

VI

FRANK BOWMAN had chosen his ranch site well when he had come here ten years or more before. The Panhandle had been almost wide open then, and he had been able to make his own choice. The northern part of his vast range was mostly open, rolling plains, with a vast sweep of grass stretching on and on, losing itself against a clear, blue sky. The southern part began with the breaks. The headquarters had been built up toward the head of a great, wide canyon. From there, the farther southward a rider went the rougher and brushier the land became.

It was to this country that cattle could drift for protection against the howling blue blizzards that would come roaring down from the high plains. Again, it was here that they could come when rainfall was short and the natural lakes went dry in the higher country. Here several springs burst forth from broken land and gave birth to welcome creeks which carried their precious water by tortuous routes through the rough country.

At near dusk, Helen Kirk turned in the seat. "We're almost there. Around that next hill, you can see it."

Rounding the hill, they heard a boy's shrill yelping and the sharp, frightened bawl of a calf. A brown and white spotted calf rushed toward them, fast as it could run. Right on its heels a young cowboy came spurring, swinging a rope over his head. The rope sailed out over the calf's shoulder and missed. The boy checked his horse's speed, disappointed. Then he saw the buck-board. He jerked up on the reins, half scared.

"Joe," Helen Kirk called sharply, "you stop running that calf. Come here!"

Head down, the boy nudged the horse with his heel and started toward them in a slow walk. Taking a long time about it, he coiled his rope, letting the loop drag on the ground behind him until he pulled it up and finished the coils.

He was ten, maybe eleven. He had a freckled face and bowl haircut, and he looked to be as full of mischief as a cat in a sewing box. One front tooth was chipped just a little.

Mrs. Kirk said firmly, "Joe, you know your dad has told you twenty times not to be running these calves and roping everything that moves."

Hanging his head, the boy answered, "Aw, Mom, I wasn't hurting anything. Besides——"

The woman cut in, her voice suddenly anxious. "Joe, what's that cut across your face?"

It was only a little scratch. "Got it chasing an old wild cow through the brush. It don't amount to nothing."

Her voice carried a world of love and worry. "You've got to be more careful, son. A thing like that could get you hurt badly. Now you follow along with us. We're going home."

Freckled Joe Kirk stared at Kenny Norwood. His mischievous brown eyes studied Kenny from head to toe, and a crooked grin broke across his wide mouth. Kenny shrank back a little.

As the buckboard rolled on into the big ranch head-quarters, Helen Kirk pointed out the various buildings. "That," she told Espy, pointing to the big rock house which stood on a small knoll, overlooking the rest of the place, "is the one Mr. Frank built. It's Mary's now.

Down there, that long half-dugout, is the bunkhouse. And next to it is the kitchen.''

Two frame houses had risen up between the old dugouts and the big rock house. ''That one nearest the bunkhouse is ours, Sam's, Joe's, and mine. Mr. Frank built it for us three years ago, and moved us out of one of the dugouts.''

She pointed, ''That other lumber building, nearest to the rock house, will be yours, I guess. It's the syndicate quarters. The lumber came down by freight wagon all the way from the railroad at Dodge City. You could have a big brick home in the city for what those two cost, with the freight and all. But a woman sets a lot of store in having a frame house instead of a dugout. Not many houses like them in this country.''

Espy nodded. For his own money he had rather have had a snug dugout than a raw house set up on blocks, at the mercy of the everlasting prairie wind. Good dugout was warmer in the winter and cooler in the summer. But, like Mrs. Kirk said, a frame house was the measure of well-being out here.

Mary Bowman stopped the buckboard in front of the house that would be Espy's and Kenny's. They unloaded it.

''I'll go down and tell the cook you're coming,'' she said. Her voice still held a chill. She flipped the reins, and the buckboard pulled away.

Mrs. Kirk went into the house with Espy and Kenny. It was almost dark. She found a lamp and lighted it. The house had only two rooms, a front room, or parlor, and a bedroom with two beds in it. Bedding was stacked on an open shelf. Mrs. Kirk pulled away a quilt. She sneezed at the settled dust which came drifting down.

''Hasn't been anyone in here since we gathered up Geoffrey Spence's belongings and shipped them to his people. You heard about Mr. Spence?''

Espy nodded.

Helen Kirk shook her head sympathetically. "He was a nice man. I can't say that for the others who came out here. Most of them have been . . . Well, they were a real burden to bear. Acted as if they were going to take over the whole place, as if no one else had any rights at all.

"That's what's really the matter with Mary. I hope you'll have patience with her. She learned to hate the others, and she can't believe that you'll be any different."

Espy's eyes met hers. "How do *you* know I will?"

The question was a little too direct. She dropped her gaze, her cheeks coloring. "I'm a pretty good judge of people, Mr. Norwood. And I like you."

She busied herself in inspecting the room. She shook her head. "It's hopeless until I get it swept out," she said. "I'll do that while you're eating supper. But first you'd better come over to our house, Mr. Norwood. I'll tend to those cuts on your face."

At the front door she paused. Embarrassed, she said, "If . . . if the boy needs to go out back, there's a lantern hanging outside, by the door."

Helen Kirk's house was built much like the other. It was bigger, with a kitchen, a bedroom, and a front room. Espy knew the wind would sometimes come whistling through the stripping of the outside walls. But a layer of bright, flowered wallpaper helped seal the house.

In one corner of the front room was a rumpled cot, evidently the boy's. Cheery curtains hung about the windows. Although dust had settled during her absence, and the cluttered kitchen showed the results of a short period of batching by a man and a boy, Espy knew the house was always expertly and lovingly kept.

Helen Kirk went into the kitchen to get some antiseptic from a cabinet. Espy looked over the furnishings. Most of them were plain, simple, and built for utility. Rawhide-bottomed chairs. Brightly-dyed throw rugs, made of strips of sacking. But there were evidences of a generous husband—a fine heavy china cabinet, and a huge Charter Oak stove.

Espy flinched against the burning of the antiseptic. Kenny, watching from a respectable distance, flinched with him. Mrs. Kirk's fingers were gentle and sure, and Espy found himself enjoying their touch, even though they brought momentary pain as she treated the abrasions on his face. Somehow he felt comfortable here. Comfortable like he had been with Jeannie, a long time ago. This home was much like their own had been.

A boy's footsteps clumped loudly on the porch outside. Young Joe Kirk shoved through the door. A little brown dog nosed right in behind him. Joe opened the door wider and gently shoved the dog back outside. "No, Slats," he said softly, "Mom's back now."

Espy saw Helen Kirk strain to hold back her laughter. But she managed to make her voice firm. "You've been letting that dog in while I've been gone, haven't you?"

"No, Mom. Well, not much, anyway."

"The woodbox is almost empty. You'd better go right on out back and bring in some more wood. I want the box full this time. Right to the brim."

Espy looked at Kenny. "You go on out and help him, son. You boys had just as well start getting acquainted."

Kenny wasn't enthusiastic about it. He held back until Espy told him a second time. Then he went out with worry in his face. Espy knew what the trouble was. Kid like Joe could throw a scare into a city boy pretty easily, if he wanted to. Joe looked as if he would probably want to.

''That's a healthy-looking son you have,'' Espy said when the boys were gone. ''Favors you some.''

She smiled. ''Thank you. But the way Joe looks right now, I don't know if that's much of a compliment or not.''

Espy said, ''He looks just like a growing cowboy ought to look. I wouldn't worry about him. Now, if he was neat and clean and quiet all the time, I *might* worry about him.''

Neat, and clean, and quiet. Like Kenny Norwood.

Mrs. Kirk replied, ''Well, Joe surely won't fit that description. But what boy wouldn't be on the wild side, way out here like this? Why, he's never even had a friend his own age to play with.''

''What about schooling?''

''I teach him. I was a schoolteacher when I met Sam.''

A happy thought struck Espy. ''Say, maybe you could teach Kenny, too. I'd pay you.''

She smiled, shaking her head. She was almost pretty when she smiled. A man never noticed her plainness the second time.

''I'd be glad to teach him, right along with Joe. And I won't take a nickel! It'll be worth it, just to get a playmate for our boy.''

When she had finished doctoring his face. Espy stood up, his hat in his hands. ''I sure do like your place here, Mrs. Kirk. It probably makes you the envy of every woman in the country. Your husband must be very good to you.''

''Sam's a good husband,'' she replied. ''I'm a lucky woman.''

Espy smiled at her, meaning exactly what he said. ''And he's a lucky man.''

The kitchen was a long half-dugout, running along

the edge of a slope, Its back wall was solid earth, where the structure had been carved out of the ground. The front was of pickets and sod. Four small windows had been placed along the long front wall. The door hung open.

Espy had to duck to walk through it. He saw the cook standing beside a big iron stove, sharpening a long butcher knife and scowling. They eyed each other for a minute. The cook was a short, slender man whose pants were two sizes too big for him and who wouldn't weigh a hundred and thirty pounds soaking wet. He looked as if he had acid in his veins instead of blood.

"You're the new syndicate man." It was a question, but the way he said it made it a stated fact. Resentment was evident in his rasp-rough voice.

Espy nodded. "I'm Espy Norwood. This is my son, Kenny."

The cook grunted. "My name's Jess Cooley." He stared in disapproval. "You're another Englishman, I guess. Well, I hope you brung your own tea with you. If you didn't, by Jasper, you ain't agonna git any."

Espy grinned then. He'd known half a hundred wagon cooks, and most of them were like this. Grouchiness was expected of them, and they generally obliged. It was more in pretense than in earnest. Let a cook get too easy and first thing he knew the cowboys would be running over him. Keep them at a distance and keep them about half boogered. That was the cook's theory. That way, he got along fine.

Espy said, "My preference runs to coffee, Jess. Black coffee, and not much water in it."

Cooley paused in his sharpening of the knife. His scowl eased. "You don't talk like the rest of them. You talk plain, sensible English."

"Maybe that's because I learned my English in Texas. I was born here."

Cooley blinked and laid down the knife. "A Texas man, by Jasper. Well now, that's an improvement."

The cook's hard shell crumbled away. He walked over and shook Espy's hand. "Miss Mary came storming in here while ago and told me to fix supper for the new syndicate man. She was too mad to talk, so I naturally figured it was another one of them kind."

Jess Cooley reached into a bucket and brought out some eggs. "Don't you let on to the cowboys, but I'll fry you some hen fruit. Mighty few outfits in this country have got a flock of laying hens. Between the coyotes and these chicken-hungry cowboys, it's all I can do to keep them."

Shortly he set down a platter of eggs and fried steak, along with some warmed-over biscuits. Kenny cleaned up two eggs and a piece of steak and asked for more, thereby earning the cook's undying friendship.

"Nothing I like better than a boy with a good appetite," he grinned, breaking another egg into his skillet. "You'll have to go some to outeat Sam Kirk's boy, though. He can get around more food than six good men."

The door swung open and a young cowboy stepped in, ducking to keep from bumping his head on the jamb. "Hey there, Greasy, what you got cooked that a man could hold down?"

Cooley scowled at him. He pulled out his shiny old pocket watch and pointed at it. "Supper's at six-thirty. You missed it. Now, Cotton Dulaney, you just hitch up your belt a notch and wait till morning."

The kid named Cotton sailed his hat into a corner, rubbing white from the gyprock plaster of the earth wall. He ate a cold biscuit, then grimaced. "A man could lose a tooth on one of these. Say, what's that, eggs? I like mine with the sunny side up."

The cook grunted, "I'll kick you out of here with

your sunny side up. How come you not to be here when you was supposed to?''

"Had an errand to run for Sam. I found somebody had chased some cattle off. I'd've trailed them myself, only Sam said no. He said just go to town and get the deputy sheriff.''

"You weren't gone long enough to get to town.''

Dulaney shook his head. His hair was almost cottony in color. Plain enough where he got his name.

"No, I just rode down to Gid's ranch and found the deputy there. He always is. Helps Gid try to drink up all the whisky that Lee & Reynolds can freight down from the railroad.''

In disgust Jess Cooley grunted, "And I reckon he promised he'd find the cattle.''

"Sure. He'll get right on it. Soon's he sobers up, about the middle of next week.''

Cooley scowled. "Someday maybe this outfit will start hunting down cow thieves instead of waiting around for a deputy sheriff that don't even know which way is up.''

He broke two more eggs into the skillet. He growled at Cotton, "You tell any of them other yahoos that I fixed you some eggs, and next time I'll just let you go hungry.''

Cotton turned to face Espy. Kidlike, he made no effort to conceal his curiosity. "What happened to you, feller? Fall out of a wagon or something?''

Espy replied, "Something like that.''

The young cowboy studied Espy's face, "Well, I hope the other feller looks worse,'' he grinned.

He jerked his thumb at Cooley. "This old horned toad's too impolite to introduce anybody. Cotton Dulaney's my name. I'm one of the top hands around here.''

Jess Cooley growled. "Top hand, my left hind foot.

He can't pour water out of a bucket if the instructions are printed on the bottom.''

Espy shook the young puncher's hand. "I'm Espy Norwood. I'm here for the syndicate."

"What's the matter," Cotton asked, "they run out of Englishmen?"

Then he frowned. "I oughtn't to've said that, I reckon. I got along fine with Geoffrey Spence. Fact is, it was me that found him . . . after the accident."

Espy looked up sharply. He filed that information away in his mind. He might want to use it later.

"You said Sam Kirk sent you for the deputy. Have you ever trailed any stolen cattle yourself?"

Cotton nodded, his mouth full of egg. "Yeah, but I lost the trail. And Sam gave me hell about it, afterwards. He's like Mr. Frank used to be. Says trailing cow thieves is a job for the law. He doesn't want any Figure 4 cowboys getting killed doing it."

"Has that ever happened?"

"No, but there was one old boy got shot in the arm a couple of years ago. Mr. Frank never did let us chase rustlers again."

Espy wondered at that. Not many ranchmen would restrain their cowboys from trailing thieves, and even administering quick justice beneath a cottonwood limb or an uptilted wagon tongue. "Does the law ever catch any?"

"Now and again. It don't do much to them, though. Tells them to leave the country and not come back. Some do, some don't."

Espy had finished his supper. He hadn't been able to eat much. Now he toyed with his coffee cup, pouring more coffee although he didn't really have a taste for it.

"Cotton," he said presently, "I'd like to have somebody show me over the ranch. Could I get you to do it?"

Behind the words was an unspoken curiosity about stolen cattle, and about things in general. Lots of time a man found out more from an observant kid cowboy than he could from the owner or even the foreman.

"Sure," Cotton said, "suits me fine. You better ask Sam Kirk first, though. After all, he's the boss."

Espy nodded. "Sure, I'll square it with him."

He knew he really wouldn't, however, not until he had come back. He didn't want anybody coaching Cotton as to what to say and what to keep quiet about.

"All right," Cotton said, pulling away from the table. "I'll be ready just as soon as this old slouch here can get breakfast in the morning."

Jess Cooley shook his butcher knife at the cowboy, his voice tough as rawhide. "You watch how you talk about your betters, boy, or I'll get you put on the wood wagon, helping old Pancho."

But he was grinning when Cotton Dulaney walked whistling out of the kitchen. "A good boy, that Cotton. He'll make a real ranch foreman someday, if he doesn't break his neck first in some kid foolishness."

Mary Bowman was waiting beside the saddle shed when Sam Kirk wearily rode in. Swinging stiffly down from his bay horse, Kirk looked at her in surprise.

"Why, hello, Mary. You sure must've hurried. Didn't expect you two back for a couple more days."

Medium tall, Sam Kirk was a few years short of forty, but he looked older. He had been handsome once, and was handsome still, in a way. He had a strong, angular face that might have been carved out of oak. There was a directness about him, and a kind of basic honesty that Mary had always liked.

He peered closer at the girl, then frowned. "What's the matter, Mary?"

She tried to keep control of herself. "Sam, they're
. . . they're . . ."

Then she was sobbing. She leaned against the pole
fence, digging her fingernails into the dead bark and
trying to choke down her emotion. Sam Kirk stepped
up beside her, placing his hands comfortingly on her
shoulders. She was thankful for his strength. Times like
this, he was almost a big brother to her. She got hold of
her voice in a minute.

"Sam, they're trying to take my ranch away from
me."

"They?" He puzzled a moment. "The syndicate?"

She nodded, her jaw setting firmly. "I'm sorry to
break down like this. All day I've been trying to hold
on, trying to be tough. The glove just won't fit."

Kirk nodded sympathetically. "Maybe you'd better
tell me about it, Mary."

She told him about Espy Norwood. "He says the
syndicate has the right to name the manager. But that
can't be, Sam, can it? This place was Dad's—Dad's
and mine—for years before the syndicate was even
heard of. What right have they got to come in here now
and take the reins right out of my hands?"

Kirk shook his head, shock evident in his voice.
"They can, Mary. It's in the contract."

"But how? How could Dad have let them do it?"

Deeply troubled, Kirk replied, "Mary, at the time,
he never dreamed . . ." He hesitated. "It's a long
story, and it's too late now to change it. One way or
another, we'll just have to make the best of it." His
voice tightened. "I promise you this—if he gets too
troublesome, Mary, I'll run him off."

She shook her head. "That's already been tried. He
didn't scare."

She told him about Quirt Wolford's reception. Kirk

stared at her in disbelief. "Mary, *you* didn't——"

"No, I didn't have anything to do with it. But next time, maybe I will."

Kirk grinned, a cold, humorless grin. "I think that glove *could* fit you, Mary. If it comes to that, I'll help you make it fit."

After turning his horse loose and hanging up his saddle, Kirk started up the slope toward his house. He glanced once at the bunkhouse, thinking he might see if Cotton Dulaney had come back. But he changed his mind. He knew the deputy. Didn't matter much whether Cotton had found him or not. Nothing would ever come of it anyway.

He found the cookstove hot and a pan of biscuits baking in the oven. But Helen was not in the house. Glancing out the window, he could see lamplight in the syndicate house. He saw Helen step out onto the little front porch and shake dust out of a blanket.

Anger rippled in him. His wife didn't have to work for them too. If they wanted to have somebody clean up for them, why didn't they bring a valet?

He eased into his tall, hard-backed rocking chair, just now realizing how tired he really was. He pulled out his watch and checked the time. He started to slip it back into his pocket, then changed his mind. For a time he studied the inscription on the back:

"To Sam Kirk, fine foreman, fine friend. From Frank Bowman."

A veil of sadness settled over him. His fingers gently caressed the silver case. It was a new watch. Mr. Frank had given it to him only a few weeks before his death.

At the sound of Helen's footsteps, Kirk slipped the watch into his pocket and stiffly pushed to his feet.

Just inside the door, Helen Kirk stopped in surprise, joy spreading over her face. "Sam. I watched for you, but I didn't see you come in. Too dark, I guess."

"I guess."

Helen's heartbeat picked up. She took an eager step forward, hoping he would take her into his arms, this time.

But Sam placed his hands on her shoulders and gave her a quick kiss on the forehead. She took hold of his hand and squeezed it hard, covering her disappointment. She gazed fondly in his face, which was baked a deep brown by a lifetime in the sun. She wanted to run her hand through his dark hair and the glistening gray that streaked it.

"Have a good trip?" he asked her.

"Fine. But I'm glad to be home, Sam. I always miss you."

He gave her a tired smile, then dropped wearily into his chair.

"You've been working too hard again, Sam," she said worriedly. "But supper'll be ready in a few minutes. You'll feel better when you eat."

He nodded. "I'm just weary, Helen, that's all. Just tired."

She turned away, pain sharpening her face. Tired. Yes, he was terribly tired. But there was more to it than that. Much more. She had been watching it build in him for more than a year now. Like some malignant growth, the worry had eaten and burned within him, deepening the furrows in his forehead, setting new strands of gray to shining in his hair.

Yet when she had tried to help him, he had always drawn away. His answer was always the same. "Just tired, Helen. Just tired."

VII

KENNY NORWOOD sat forlornly alone in the little frame house which was to be his home. His throat was tight, and he had fought hard to keep from sobbing in his loneliness. Looking about him in the raw, barren little room, he remembered the house where he had lived so long in Kansas City, the huge brick house with its massive furniture, its deep rugs, and the big windows which seemed to bring everything right indoors.

He had grown used to the noise which was always part of a city, even the residential areas. There were always the servants moving about downstairs, or back in the kitchen. Here there was nothing. No sound except the prairie wind whistling through a crack in the wall, and somewhere out yonder the melancholy bawling of a cow whose calf had been butchered for meat.

Espy had gotten the boy up before daylight and had taken him down to the dugout cookshack. Kenny had shrunk back from the bearded, rough-talking cowboys. He had disliked the way they all eyed him and his clean clothes with their city cut. He had winced when the one called Cotton had laughingly accused him of being a little Englishman.

"Don't let them get your goat, son," Espy had smiled later. "It's cowboy nature to hooraw a kid. They don't mean anything by it. Show them you can take it, and they'll do anything in the world for you."

Kenny hadn't answered him, for he still felt ill at ease even with his father. A stubborn resentment clung to him whenever his mind drifted back to Kansas City, and the comfortable home from which his father had dragged him.

But, even so, he had had to fight back a helpless panic when his father had saddled a horse this morning and ridden southward with the young cowboy, Cotton.

"We may be late getting back, son," Espy had said. "When it comes dinnertime, you just go on over to the cookshack. You might as well look the place over today, and get acquainted."

Kenny hadn't done much looking. Soon after his father left, he had high-tailed it back to the house. Now he sat there alone, sick at heart, loneliness a dull ache in him. He wished for a friendly word from somebody. Anybody.

It was Mrs. Kirk who brought it. She came over with a mop and a broom under her arm and a bucket of water in her hand.

"Why, Kenny," she said in surprise, "Whatever are you doing sitting here all by yourself? It's a pretty morning. You ought to go outside and play."

Kenny instinctively liked this woman. He liked the way she smiled at him, and patted him on the head. Somewhere, far back in his memory, was a vague picture of another woman who had done that way. It had been a long time ago. He couldn't remember exactly what she looked like. But he remembered the softness of her voice when she spoke to him, and the way she smiled at him and ran her hand through his hair. Aunt Margaret had loved him, he knew that, but she hadn't been given to this kind of tenderness. It was not fitting for a person of dignity, she had once said.

"My Joe's playing out around the barn," Mrs. Kirk told Kenny. "Why don't you go out and find him? You two boys can have a lot of fun together, once you get acquainted."

Heart heavy with misgivings, Kenny left the house. He didn't think he liked Joe. He hadn't liked the way the boy had stared at him last night when they were packing in wood. Kenny turned once and looked back to see Mrs. Kirk sweeping dirt through the front door. With halting steps he moved on out to the barn. His heart was tripping with every step he took. He was like a frightened rabbit, ready to sprint for the brush.

"You look like a sissy to me!"

The voice hauled him up short. He spun on his heel. Joe Kirk was watching him from the top of a big stack of lake hay.

Joe leered belligerently at him for a full minute before he slid down in a dusty shower of hay and came striding forward, barefoot. Kenny froze. He thought of the boys he had known in private school. None of them looked like this.

The freckled boy stopped an arm's length from him and stood there regarding him solemnly, his hands on his hips. His mouth was open so Kenny could see where one front tooth was chipped a little. Kenny's heart was thumping.

"Hello," he managed to say.

"I betcha I can whip you," Joe said.

Kenny's tongue flicked out over his dry lips. "Your mother said I should come down here and get acquainted with you."

Joe wasn't going to be sidetracked. "Don't you think I can whip you?"

Kenny didn't know what to do. He had never run into a situation like this. Joe Kirk didn't look any bigger than Kenny Norwood. But the thought of a fist fight made Kenny shrink back.

"Fisticuffs are for common young ruffians," Aunt Margaret had scolded him once after he and another little boy had shoved each other into a hole of mud. Kenny had won that fight. But this one . . .

"Come on, dude," Joe Kirk challenged, bringing up his hard little fists. "Put up your dukes."

Kenny took a step backward. Joe followed him.

Then, courage leaving him, Kenny turned and ran, out past the bar and on toward the corrals that stretched beyond it. He ran and ran, and kept running until his lungs were ready to burst.

He stopped finally, humiliation spilling through him in a flood. He sat down on the ground there, chest aheave, a desperate loneliness gripping him. And with it came a rising anger at himself, at Joe Kirk, at his father, at this whole wild country.

Far behind him, Joe Kirk stood with hands on his hips, jeering at him.

"Fraidy cat! Fraidy cat!"

A predawn start and a steady, mile-eating trot carried Espy Norwood and Cotton Dulaney to the south end of Frank Norwood's Figure 4 range by late morning. Down here it was rougher country than that farther north. It was still good grass land, but it was chopped by running creeks, by dry creek beds, and by sudden canyons with steep walls that pitched downward to rocky, broken floors. Lacing back and forth across all of it were the brushy thickets, mesquite, cedar, and in places wild china and hackberries.

Once they topped a rise and flushed a little bunch of antelope, grazing the strong, short grass. Laughing, Cotton Dulaney stepped out of the saddle and pulled his saddle gun out of its scabbard in one quick motion.

Espy wanted to stop him, hating to see anything killed without reason. But he held still, yesterday's soreness slowing him.

Cotton dropped to one knee and took careful aim at the flash of a broad white tail. The gun clicked harmlessly.

The young cowboy arose with a grin. "I don't ever really shoot them, not unless we need the meat. I just get a big kick out of knowing I could, if I wanted to."

Espy grinned with him, and a new sense of relief eased through him. He really liked this kid cowboy now. Cotton might still have his share of wild oats, but beneath it all was a basic horse sense that steadied him. He would be a really good man bye and bye, when the kid in him had worn itself away.

"Not far from here to the south line camp," Cotton said, pointing westward. "I had taken a string of horses over there and was on my way back when I cut the sign."

"Follow it far?"

"Just far enough to be sure I wasn't wrong. Last time I followed a bunch like that, Sam Kirk chewed me out so that my ears rang for a week. The way he sees it, I'm still just a kid."

A spark of humor played in Espy's gray eyes. "How old *are* you?"

"I'm . . . well, I'll be twenty-one my next birthday."

"And how long is that?"

Cotton colored. "Not quite a year."

Not much was left of the tracks. They were three days old, maybe four. Hard to tell anymore how many cattle there had been. Thirty head. Maybe forty.

A cold, hard anger began to grow in Espy, the anger that thieves always aroused. "Let's follow the trail a ways. See where they headed."

Cotton was more than ready. Grinning, he drew his six-gun and checked the load in the cylinder.

Espy shook his head. "Put that thing up, son. The

trail's old. If I thought we'd run into anything dangerous, I wouldn't take you."

Cotton put the gun back where it belonged. The two
rode along the old trail in silence, watching the ground.

Espy remarked, "Frank Bowman must not have
been very worried about cow thieves, or he wouldn't
have left it all to some sorry deputy."

Cotton shook his head. "I'm afraid Mr. Frank never
realized how many cattle were being hazed off down
into this brush country. His health got bad, and he never
rode much the last couple of years. Never saw it for
himself."

"Were there many cattle lost?"

Cotton said, "I've been working for this outfit for
three years. I can tell. There aren't as many cattle down
here as there used to be. It shows up some at branding
time. Doesn't take as long to brand out a camp and
move the chuckwagon as it used to."

After an hour or so, the dim, blown-out trail led
down into a creek. It didn't come out on the other side.

"Driving them in the water to kill the trail," Espy
commented.

They followed the crooked creek an hour. Finally
Espy reined up, shaking his head in slow anger. "They
came out back up the creek somewhere. We missed it.
Probably on one of those dry, rocky creek beds."

Without having to ask, he knew it would be easy for
rustlers to get away with cattle once they got them down
here to the rough country. There would be hundreds of
places they could hide livestock. And from here there
were several directions they could go to market them
—northeast to the Oklahoma country, east to the settled
parts of Texas, or west across the Panhandle to New
Mexico.

"We'd just as well head back, Cotton," he said.

He knew it had been futile, following this old trail.

But it had satisfied his curiosity. And it had fanned up an anger.

"Nobody's followed this trail but us," he told Cotton when they again reached the point where it had led into the creek. "No horse tracks but ours."

Cotton spat disgustedly. "Like I said, that deputy's probably still over there helping Gid drink up his whisky."

Espy's fist knotted. "How far is it to this Gid's place?"

Cotton's eyes widened, and he began to grin in anticipation, "From right here, it's three or four miles. We can be there before you know it."

"All right, then. Let's go."

Espy's face twisted as soon as he saw the place, and he spat disgustedly. "Looks like an old boar's nest," he muttered.

Not a single building stood much above ground level. The barn was no barn at all, but only a dugout shed in front of disintegrating pole corrals which had been thrown up with mesquite and cedar. It faced toward a larger dugout, carved into the side of a hill. This one obviously was home for the ranch owner. A tin chimney shoved up out of a sod-covered roof. Most of the structure was below ground level. There was just room enough for one small window between the ground and the roof. A set of steps led down to the door.

A man stood on these steps. As Espy and Cotton rode in, he quickly ducked through the door and out of sight. But not so quickly that Espy did not get a sudden impression of wide shoulders and coal-black whiskers. Quirt Wolford? Maybe, maybe not. But excitement began to play through him.

"Cotton," he asked, "who is this Gid?"

Cotton dropped his head. "I kind of hate to tell you. Every family's apt to have a black sheep in it, some

time or other. Mr. Frank's family too. Gid Bowman is
Frank Bowman's brother.''

Gid Bowman's place was like a bad taste in the
mouth. Everything about ready to fall in. A careless
scattering of tin cans and bottles and trash all over.
More bottles than anything else.

"What does he do to make a living?" Espy asked in a
low voice.

Cotton grunted. "He has a few cattle. Mostly he just
sponges off of Mr. Frank. Or did. I don't know what
he'll do now."

They stepped down. Espy looped his reins around
one wheel of an old broken-down wagon which was
slowly falling to pieces under the relentless weathering
of sun and wind and rain. Cotton followed suit, then
turned toward the steps.

"Hey there, Gid," Cotton hollered.

A rusty-colored head appeared in the doorway. The
man stood there hatless, squinting at the two visitors.
Espy took a close look at him, and surprise hit him like
a club across the shoulders.

Gid Bowman was the drunken man he had seen at
Mobeetie that night in the hotel. He was the man who
had walked in with Quirt Wolford, and tried to talk to
Mary Bowman.

Several loose strings were beginning to tie up into
one piece.

"Howdy, Gid," Cotton said. "We're looking for
Llewellyn."

Bowman was staring up at Espy, his gaze raking him
from boot heels to hat. After a moment he said, "The
new syndicate man, ain't you?"

"How did you know?"

Gid Bowman only grinned crookedly. He took a step
back into the dugout. "Llewellyn's in here, if you want
him. But he don't feel so good."

A prescient tingle worked down the back of Espy's neck. That might have been Quirt Wolford he had seen, or it might not. His hand was close to his gun as he walked down the plank steps. The boards were rotted. One of them sagged dangerously under his weight.

The stench of the dugout slapped him across the face like a sweaty saddle blanket. The air was heavy and thick with the mingled smells of cheap whisky and tobacco, man-sweat and burned food.

Espy's gaze instantly swept the little room which had been dug into a hillside. No sign of Quirt Wolford. He could have been wrong, he admitted to himself. That could have been Gid Bowman he had seen.

There was little furniture. Two rumpled, smelly cots. A few cluttered shelves. A two-lid bachelor stove with a drum inserted around the stovepipe to serve as an oven. Espy saw a small door at the back of the room, a door which could only lead back into the earth from which the dugout was cut. Probably it hid a pantry.

The deputy appeared lifeless, slumped in a chair pulled up to a stained table. His face was flushed against the pale, washed-out blue of his eyes. The long fingers of his right hand toyed listlessly with an almost-empty glass. He looked past Espy to the young Figure 4 cowboy.

"Awright, Cotton," he mumbled, "what is it now?"

Espy spoke for Cotton. His words bore the keen edge of his anger. "Cotton told you about some stolen cattle yesterday. We want to know what you found out."

The deputy shook his head. "I didn't find out nothing. Followed the tracks, but they played out. Too old."

Espy's voice cracked like a whip. "You're a liar!"

The deputy straightened and tried to focus his gaze

on Espy's face. He drew in a sharp, quick breath. "Now you looky here, stranger . . ."

Gid Bowman broke in, his face clouded. "Listen, syndicate man, you can do what you want to on my brother's place, but this outfit is mine."

Espy's eyes were still on the deputy. "You're a liar," he repeated sharply. "You never made any effort to follow that trail. You never even left this place."

In drunken rage the deputy swayed to his feet and made a clumsy effort to draw his gun. Espy jerked it out of his hand. He gave Llewellyn a shove that sent him floundering backward into his chair. He hurled the gun through the little window. The dirty glass shattered.

Shaken and scared, the deputy was suddenly half sober.

Espy faced him, his breath coming rapidly. "I haven't got any control over the county government, Llewellyn," he said flatly. "But if I were you, I'd turn in my badge and move on along. Don't ever let me see you again, because every time I see you, I'm going to kick you right in the seat of the britches. I won't care where it is, or who sees it. I'll kick your lazy rump so hard you can't sit down for a week and a half."

Llewellyn made no answer. He just sat there with chin sagging, hands aquiver.

Sullen defiance glared out of Gid Bowman's red-veined eyes. "A little overbearing, aren't you, Norwood? You forget that this is *my* place, not yours. Now you better leave."

Espy nodded, his blood still aboil. "All right, Bowman. But I want you to know one thing. From now on the Figure 4 is my responsibility. If we ever need a deputy again, we'd better not find him over here, drunk. Let it happen again and I'll pull this boar's nest right down around your ears. Let's go, Cotton!"

As he turned sharply toward the door, his angry gaze fell upon an open letter lying on a dusty shelf. He knew that handwriting. Espy picked up the letter. It was from Colonel Judkins. And it was addressed to Mary Bowman. Without having to read it, he knew what letter it was.

Shoving it into his pocket, he stalked out, the grinning young cowboy two steps behind him. Outside, Espy stopped so abruptly that Cotton bumped into him. He was looking beyond the barn. "My mules," he exclaimed.

Walking toward the dugout barn in their free-swinging gait were the two mules he had bought in Dodge City, the two Quirt Wolford and his men had driven off yesterday.

Espy whirled back, facing the surprised Gid Bowman. "Those are my mules. What are they doing here?"

Bowman was suddenly flustered, his anger shoved aside. "*Your* mules?" Then, shrugging his shoulders, he said. "They strayed into camp this morning. I didn't know the brand on them, so I left them alone."

Espy stared hard at him. He knew within reason that the man was lying. "I'm taking them with me."

Bowman shrugged again. "Sure. Sure, if they're your mules, then take them on along."

The rusty-haired, short-bearded man stood in the doorway, his nerves tingling, watching Espy Norwood and Cotton spur northward, driving the mules ahead of them. He stepped back into the dugout and sighed.

The pantry door swung open, and a man moved out from his hiding place behind it. He was a broad-shouldered man with hair black as an Indian's, his face almost hidden behind a stubble of black, coarse beard.

Gid Bowman glanced at him, then sagged into a

chair and poured a glass partly full from a bottle at the table. He downed it in one gulp.

"Damn it, Quirt," he said sharply, frowning at the whisky's fire, "you ought to've shot them mules. Mistake like that could spill all the beans in the pot."

Wolford growled. "Them mules was too good to shoot. They'd be worth a right smart of money. I aimed to send them west and sell them."

Bowman poured another drink. He glanced at the half-sobered deputy, then at Wolford's bruised, swollen face. "That Norwood's a tough man. I can see now how he whipped you."

Wolford jerked his head around in sudden fury and slammed his gun onto the table. He had held it in his hand the whole time he had stood behind the door. "He *didn't* whip me, Gid. You got that? He *didn't* whip me."

Bowman shrugged, fingering his glass. "Have it your way. All I know is what the boys said."

Wolford sat down, nursing his anger. He toyed with the gun. "I could've shot him while ago, right through the door. He'd never've known what hit him."

Gid Bowman frowned. "Be patient, Quirt. Maybe you'll have to do it yet."

VIII

THE KANSAS CITY streets rumbled with activity this warm summer afternoon. But Margaret Tellison's driver was a good one, and he maneuvered her carriage expertly through the trying tangle of horses, vehicles, and foot traffic. Presently he pulled over to the curb in front of the dressmaker's shop and in studied deference helped Margaret down from the carriage.

"You may go now, Stevens," she said. "I shall be ready at four o'clock."

"Yes, Mrs. Tellison." The driver tipped his hat, climbed back into the carriage, and eased it out into the busy street.

Margaret Tellison stepped up to the door of the shop and waited there. When she knew the driver was out of sight of her, she moved out upon the brick sidewalk again and walked briskly around the corner, nervously twirling her parasol in black-gloved hands.

She saw the man she expected, leaning lazily against a brightly-painted carriage, idly twirling a gold chain. He was expensively dressed, a little on the flashy side. Seeing her, he straightened.

"You found him?" she asked quickly.

He nodded. "I found him."

Impatience sharpened her voice. "Where is he, then? Why didn't you bring him?"

Dan Carver grunted. "Man like him is as independent as a hog on ice, Mrs. Tellison. He don't go running just because somebody wants to see him. He says if you've got business, you can go to him. He won't come to you."

She tapped the parasol handle impatiently against her palm, her lips tightening. "Very well, I'll go. Do you know where he is?"

Carver nodded. "I've got my rig here. "I'll take you."

Hand on her elbow, he gave her a lift into the back seat of his double carriage. Margaret Tellison quickly looked about her, hoping she was not being watched by anyone who knew her. Her wide hat had a black veil. She pulled it down over her face for what protection it might give her against recognition. Then she sank deep into the seat while Carver flipped his whip at the team and pulled out into the horsedrawn traffic.

Revulsion brought a tremor to her as she looked at the back of Carver's fat neck. To think that Mrs. Edgar Tellison should ever have to conduct business with a man of this type, and of the type of the man to whom Carver was taking her.

Once a Kansas City police officer, Carver had been caught taking his share of bribe money from a well-known madam of the city. Not that such bribery was an unusual occurrence, but most policemen were discreet enough not to get caught at it. Now Carver continued to do work of a police type on a private basis. Suspicious wives sent him on the trail of errant husbands. Gamblers sent him to search for debtors who had left town without mentioning their destination. Politicians paid him well for digging up useful slander against their opponents.

For Margeret Tellison, he had found out where Espy Norwood had gone with his son. Now he had found a man who nursed a burning hatred of Espy.

Margaret's frown deepened as the carriage took her

into the bawdier section of the city. Nervously she fingered the veil and wished it were heavier.

Carver finally pulled the carriage up in front of a nondescript two-story frame hotel. Margaret accepted his help in stepping down. She felt her face warming under the shameless stare of two rumpled-looking men slouched on a bench in front.

"I'll go in with you," Carver offered.

She shook her head quickly. "No. You wait out here."

The first time she had seen Carver she had had a disturbing thought that the payment for a detective service rendered might be only the first in an endless series of payments. She had had imagination enough to realize how ideal his situation was for eventual and eternal blackmail. That Carver would stoop to blackmail, she had not the slightest doubt. The best way to keep him honest, then, was to let him know as little as possible of her plans.

A balding, seedy little man sat behind the hotel desk, reading an old newspaper. He lowered the paper and stared at Margaret Tellison.

"I'm looking for a Mr. Ollinger," she said. "Matt Ollinger."

He gave her a long and thorough look before he answered, his eyes starting low and working up. Then he jerked his head toward the stairs. "Room two-twelve. Just go on up."

From the sly grin which creased his face, she guessed what he was thinking. Flame rose in her cheeks. "I'll see him down here," she said shortly. "Go get him."

He made no move until she told him the second time. "All right, all right," he said. "Just set yourself down there. I'll go."

An uncomfortable chill shook Margaret's thin shoulders as she watched Matt Ollinger walk heavily

down the stairs. He was about what she had expected.
Worse, perhaps. A dull fear began to beat in her as his
bottomless eyes touched her. His rough black beard and
his dark scowl made her think uncomfortably of a bear.

"You the woman that wanted to see me?" he demanded.

Swallowing, she nodded. She looked at the hotel
clerk, then back to Ollinger. "I want to talk to you in
private."

He led her into a small dining room that was almost
stifling with the clinging odor of burned grease. At this
time of day it was not in use. He let her pull out her own
chair, seating himself across the table where he could
look at her.

"All right, now," he spoke roughly, "what is it?"

Not quite sure of herself, Margaret began, "I understand you've had some trouble with a man named Espy
Norwood."

His eyes cut back to sudden narrowness, and his big
fist clenched on the table. He leaned forward angrily,
half rising.

"If you've come to talk to me about Espy Norwood,
you'd just as well leave."

"Wait," she said anxiously, "I have an offer to
make."

He eased back into his chair, his fist still clenched.

Hurriedly she went on. "I've had trouble with him,
too. I know a way you can even up for both of us, and
make some money as well."

He listened with interest while she told him about
Espy's taking Kenny away.

"Now I've found out where he's gone," she said.

His eyes widened, and his jaw squared. "Where?"

"Texas."

Ollinger's hand eased back from the table, near the
butt of the gun he wore at his hip. He looked past

Margaret Tellison, some violent dream building behind his washed-out eyes.

"Texas," he spoke softly. "It'd almost be worth a ride down there . . ."

He dropped it at that. His gaze returned to the woman. "What's this proposition you were talking about?"

"I'll give you five hundred dollars to steal that boy from him for me."

Pleasure warmed Ollinger's dark face. "You got you a deal. I'll get the boy for you. And I'll get Espy Norwood while I'm at it."

Her eyes went wide with fear. "No, no, nothing like that. I don't want Espy hurt. Just get the boy back. That's all I want."

"But we couldn't just let Norwood alone," he argued. "What's to keep him from coming right back up here and taking the button away from you again?"

Confidently she answered. "I have a lot of influence in this town. Once I get Kenny back here, the law will help me keep him. I'll show the court that Espy Norwood is unfit to rear a boy. I'll have him sent to jail if he even so much as tries to *see* Kenny again."

Ollinger eyed her with curiosity. "What else did this Norwood do to you—even before he took the boy away?"

Her breath cut short. "What do you mean?"

"He must have done something else to you. I see it in your eyes. Did he ever jilt you or something?"

She recoiled as if he had hit her. Her cheeks flamed. She tried to say something, but it didn't come out.

He shrugged. "Forget it. None of my business, I reckon. Just how do you want me to handle this job?"

After a time she got a tight rein on her anger. "I don't care, so long as you don't shoot anybody. Just get Kenny to me in Mobeetie. I'll wait there."

Ollinger rubbed his whiskered chin. "Why don't I bring him all the way back to Kansas City? I wouldn't charge you much more for that. Say two-fifty."

She shook her head. She had considered that possibility when she had first come upon the whole idea. But the thought of gently-reared Kenny having to spend days or weeks in the care of this ruffian . . .

She said, "No, I'll go to Mobeetie and wait. I'll pay you when you bring the boy to me."

"All right. Any way you want to do it. What does your husband think about this, Mrs. Tellison?"

In alarm she said, "He mustn't know anything of it, not until it's over. I'll tell him I'm going to Chicago to spend a few weeks."

Ollinger nodded. "But I'd still like to take care of Norwood."

"No," she repeated strongly. "I don't want him killed. You have to promise me you won't hurt him. That's part of the deal."

Ollinger gave in easily enough. "Sure," he shrugged. "it's your money. If stealing his boy is all the revenge you want, then that's where we stop."

Margaret Tellison was glad to be through, to be able to leave this somber man whose black reputation had reached over half of the West. She was glad to be able to get out of this evil building, and away from the baldish clerk whose beady eyes dwelt so indecently upon her.

Through a window Matt Ollinger watched her step hurriedly into Dan Carver's carriage, and watched the carriage pull away. He drew his gun. His fingers roved lovingly over it while the corners of his mouth pulled upward. The clerk walked in and leaned lazily against the doorjamb.

"Good-looking woman, Matt," he said. "If it'd been me, I wouldn't've let her get away."

"Good-looking women come cheap. This one was strictly business."

"What're you going to do?"

"I'm going to earn me five hundred dollars." He aimed the gun at a picture on the wall, smiling harshly. "And then, when I've got that money in my pocket, I'm going to pay a man off. Pay him for seven hundred and thirty steers!"

IX

A SMOKY dusk had settled when Espy Norwood and Cotton Dulaney rode up to the Figure 4 barns and hazed the two little mules into a corral. Stiff, Espy swung down. A deep soreness still lay in him from the beating he had taken the day before.

"I'll unsaddle your horse for you," Cotton offered, seeing Espy's bone-weariness.

Espy nodded, leaning against the fence. "I'd be much obliged."

A man stepped out of the barn and walked leisurely toward them.

"Howdy, Sam," Cotton greeted him, letting Espy's saddle slide to the ground while he slipped the bridle off and turned the horse loose.

"Evening, Cotton," Sam Kirk replied. He walked on up to Espy. He extended his hand. "Mr. Norwood? I'm Sam Kirk. You all got out so early this morning, I didn't get a chance to meet you."

Espy measured the ranch foreman with his eyes and was not displeased by what he saw. There's something about a real stockman that another stockman can tell as far as he can see. Espy saw it in Sam Kirk.

"Glad to know you, Sam." This was his bid for friendship, the immediate use of Kirk's first name. It was not said in the patronizing tone of a man toward those he believes to be his inferiors, the way some men would talk to a bootblack.

Kirk glanced back toward the kid cowboy. "Cotton,

the next time you go off like this, I wish you'd tell me. I'd figured on sending you to the Todd line camp today."

Espy spoke for Cotton. "I asked Cotton to show me over part of the ranch. I'd intended to tell you about it, but I never got the chance."

That was a little of a lie, and Espy had a feeling that Kirk knew it.

"Where did you go?"

"Over part of the south end."

Cotton piped up. "We took a look at those cow tracks I was telling you about, Sam. We followed them but didn't jump nothing. Then we went over to Gid's place and found Mr. Norwood's mules. You ought to've seen——"

Kirk stiffened. "You followed those tracks?"

Cotton's face fell with sudden uncertainty. "Yeah. I figured that with Mr. Norwood along, it ought to be all right."

Hands on his hips, Kirk stalked up to Cotton. His voice was tight with anger. "Kid, if I've told you once, I've told you ten times. Don't you ever go following stolen cattle like that. Those cow thieves are a desperate bunch, don't you know that? They'll put a bullet in your back. They'll leave you lying in a mesquite thicket, and nobody'll ever find you but the coyotes.

"If you can't follow orders, then you can't work for me. One more time, Cotton. One more time and you'll just have to hunt you a new job!"

Cotton's head bent downward, and his face darkened with shame. "All right, Sam. I'll remember."

Cotton carried his and Espy's saddles into the barn. "See you tomorrow, Mr. Norwood," he said in a subdued voice.

"All right, Cotton," Espy answered. When the boy was gone, he turned back to Sam Kirk. "You were a little rough on him, Sam. I wish you'd taken that out on me instead. After all, it was me that asked him to go."

Kirk shook his head firmly. "I like that boy, Norwood. That's why I was rough on him. He's a good kid, but he's got a reckless streak in him that could get him killed. I'll be just as rough on him as necessary to keep that from happening. He knew better. And you're a grown man, Norwood. You ought to've known better too."

Espy straightened. "There wasn't any danger down there, Sam. If I'd thought there was, I'd never have taken the kid."

"How could you know there wasn't any danger?" Kirk demanded. "You're a stranger here. You might-'ve ridden into an ambush. And you'd've gotten that kid killed right along with you.

"There's one thing I want understood, Norwood. It's none of my business what you do, yourself. But I don't want you getting my cowboys killed."

Espy's gray eyes narrowed. His voice sharpened to a finer edge. "I hate having to remind you, Sam, but I'm the manager here now. The syndicate sent me down here with full authority. I'll use it if I have to, till I find out how things stand."

Kirk still faced him, hands on his hips. "And I'll remind *you*, Norwood. A manager's job is to make decisions. It's up to the foreman to handle the men. I'm the foreman here. And as long as I am, *I'll* be the one who tells the men where they're to go, and what they're to do."

The two men stood there, their eyes challenging each other. Kirk's belligerence was a surprise to Espy. He knew instinctively that it hadn't flared on the spur of the moment. It must have been the result of a long building-up.

An impulse moved in Espy. Fire him right now, it

said. Fire him right now and save yourself a heap of trouble. But he managed to hold his tongue. He thought of Mrs. Kirk. He had liked that woman. For her sake, then, he would wait—and watch.

"All right, Sam. Bossing the men is your job, and I'll respect it. But I'll tell you this. If I see a man doing something I don't like, I'll fire him."

Kirk stared levelly at him a moment before he answered. "Fair enough, Norwood. I reckon we'll get along."

Espy raised his hand, but he was too late for Kirk to clasp it. Kirk already had turned and started walking up the slope toward the lamplight which shone a welcome in the windows of his frame house.

Espy frowned and kicked at a small rock which lay in the dust at his feet. This whole thing had turned out cock-eyed. Bad enough to be on the outs with the woman who owned a half-interest in the ranch. Now to make it worse, he had to get off on the wrong foot with the foreman.

He looked toward the frame house which was his. It was dark. He glanced at the friendly glow of lamplight in the Kirk house. He knew a sudden envy of Sam Kirk, and a momentary loneliness took him.

He shrugged then and set out wearily for the kitchen.

Kenny sat at one end of the long table in the dugout cookshack, morosely watching the cook put the washed and dried supper dishes back onto the open shelves.

"Did you enjoy yourself today, son?" Espy asked him.

Kenny never answered, and that was answer enough.

Cotton Dulaney sat in silence, eating a warmed-over supper, his shoulders hunched and his head low over the plate.

Hand on Cotton's shoulder, Espy said, "Sorry I got

you that chewing-out. I wouldn't have had it happen for the world.''

Soberly Cotton said, "Wasn't your fault, Mr. Norwood. Sam just can't see that I'm grown. He figures I'm due a scolding now and again, like a little old puppy.''

Espy smiled. "You just hang on. He'll see things differently, if you give him time enough.''

Later, in the syndicate house, Espy tried without luck to get Kenny to tell what he had seen and done during the day. He had just as well have tried to talk to a sorrel colt. Kenny answered him only when he asked a direct question, and the answers were short. "Yes," or "No," or "I guess so."

But Espy could see the bitter frost of unhappiness which lay in the boy's gray eyes. He finally gave up trying to talk to Kenny. Frowning worriedly, he turned away and began digging into the duplicate Figure 4 record books the colonel had sent with him.

Long after Kenny went to bed, Espy bent over the tally books, figuring with a stub pencil under the flickering glow of a kerosene table lamp.

Yes sir, they tallied up a hundred per cent, any way he went at them. Correct right down to a T.

Yet there was something here which caused the rat-gnaw of uncertainty in him. These records didn't show the kind of reduction in numbers that Cotton Dulaney had described. Sure, Cotton was just a kid, and kids let their imagination run away with them sometimes. But he was an observant button; Espy had seen that.

Next morning, after breakfast, Espy watched the big house until he knew Mary Bowman was up and about. He saw the slender girl step down off her back porch and shake out a tablecloth. Smiling, she folded the cloth against the full apron she wore and watched the cook's chickens running to grab the crumbs.

Espy felt a stirring of pleasure. There was a fresh prettiness to this girl, a prettiness he found hard to associate with men like Quirt Wolford and Gid Bowman. She looked like a happy young housewife this morning—yes, like Helen Kirk. She didn't look like a girl who two days ago had sent a brutal half-outlaw like Wolford to beat a man senseless and try to run him out of the country.

She was still wearing the apron when she answered his knock on the front door. Her friendly eyes hardened as she saw him standing there.

"Oh. Good morning, Mr. Norwood." Her voice was crisp.

Man might as well *try* to be friendly, Espy decided.

Smiling, he said. "You sure look domestic today."

She never eased up a bit. "I'm awfully busy. Is that all you came to say, or are you here on business?"

Espy began to redden. "Business, Miss Bowman."

She stepped aside and beckoned him to come into the house. She watched him like a tired store clerk being painfully civil to a customer he wishes would finish his business and get out.

Espy decided to make one more try for a truce. "Look, Miss Bowman, I don't like us to be at odds with each other, and I don't expect you do, either. I didn't know I was shoving you out of a job you thought was yours. I'm sorry it happened that way. But there's not much we can do about it now except take things the way they are and make the best of them.

"We could get along fine, and I'd like to try. What say we just mark off our grievances and start fresh?"

She rubbed her hands together thoughtfully a long moment, looking out the open door. Then she turned, a sign of humor in her face. "All right, Mr. Norwood, I'll give it a try."

Espy smiled. "Fine. And from now on it's not Mr. Norwood. It's Espy."

A wariness still showed in her eyes, but she said, "How about some coffee to seal the bargain over? There's some on the stove in the kitchen."

She was back in half a minute, carrying cups and a pot of coffee. She had removed the apron.

Sipping the coffee, Espy caught himself enjoying the sight of her, the gentle curves and soft roundness which filled the upper part of her high-buttoned house dress, narrowing down to a tiny waist before losing its form in the full flow of ankle-length skirt.

"You said you had business," she reminded him shortly.

He nodded, pointing his chin toward a roll-top desk in one corner of the room. "I wondered if I could borrow your dad's records and tally books awhile. I'd like to go over them."

"That'd be all right, I guess. But he sent the syndicate complete copies of all of them."

Espy began to squirm in discomfort. "I know."

For a time she stared at him, her eyebrows knitting. She set down her coffee cup and saucer so hard that they rattled.

"So that's it." Her voice tightened again. "You want to see if the syndicate was sent false copies. Well, I can assure you it was not, Mr. Norwood. They are exact copies of the books Dad kept."

Espy faltered. "Miss Bowman, I didn't mean it that way."

"How else could you have meant it?" Anger leapt into her eyes. "You came over here talking truce, then the first thing you did was imply that we've been cheating the syndicate with false records."

"I didn't say that. I didn't say that at all."

"You didn't have to. You made it plain enough."

In quick strides she marched to the desk, rolled up the top, and grabbed up four ledger books. She shoved them toward Espy, almost throwing them at him.

"Here they are, all of them. Check them all you want to. You won't find a mistake. But *you've* made a mistake, Norwood. You make your mistake in ever coming out here."

Espy didn't want to be angry with her. But now the heat began to crackle in him. He reached in his shirt pocket and pulled out the letter he had found at Gid Bowman's.

"You tried hard enough to convince me of that when you sicked Quirt Wolford onto me."

Her eyes widened. "I put Quirt Wolford onto you? That's a lie, Norwood. I didn't even know you were coming till you were in Mobeetie."

Espy's jaw clenched. "You told me that. You said you didn't get the colonel's letter. But I found it. It was in your Uncle Gid's dugout. How did it get over there unless you sent it? And your uncle is a friend of Quirt Wolford. It all adds up pretty handily, Miss Bowman."

She grabbed the letter. Her face colored deeply as she glanced over it and saw what it was.

"I didn't send this to my uncle. I never even saw it before."

He stared levelly at her. "You're a very pretty girl, Miss Bowman. But I learned a lesson about pretty girls a long time ago. The reddest roses have always got the sharpest thorns."

Her hands trembled, and her lips were tight as a bowstring. "Get out, Norwood," she gritted, pointing at the door. "Get out before I throw something at you and break it."

Seething, she stood in the doorway, watching him stomp along the footworn path leading down the slope.

He carried her father's record books under his arm. His back was rigid and straight as a poker.

Mary Bowman whirled on her heel. She grabbed a coffee cup and hurled it. It smashed on a doorjamb, sending a brown trickle of coffee running down to the floor.

A portly old Mexican woman came hurrying into the room, her eyes bulging with concern. She saw the smashed cup, then looked questioningly toward Mary Bowman.

"*Es nada*, Delfina," Mary said in a low voice, suddenly shamed by her uncontrolled anger. "It's nothing."

As the old woman left the room, Mary once again looked at the letter, puzzlement in her worried frown.

But her wonder over the letter quickly gave way to the fury which still smoldered beneath the surface. She looked out the window toward the syndicate house down the slope.

"You'd better watch yourself, Espy Norwood," she breathed. "One way or another, I'll get you!"

X

ESPY NORWOOD and his son Kenny had no particular trouble in finding what was known as the Todd line camp. The prairie wind was warm in their faces. The morning sun was hot and high, the shadows edging closer under the two easy-trotting horses, showing that it was only an hour or so until noon.

Espy glanced around often to look at the boy, who usually trailed a half length behind. It had surprised him a little when Kenny had decided to go with him.

"Tired, son?" he asked.

Kenny shook his head, but the sag of his young face showed that he was. He squirmed one way, then another, obviously sore and saddle-rubbed. An easy smile lifted the heaviness from Espy's countenance. Once over his soreness this time, Kenny would be all right from now on.

The Todd camp, on the upper part of Figure 4 range, was a small picket house, picket shed, and a set of pole corrals, built upon a gentle knoll amid a broad, rolling vista of short grass. It faced down toward a big shallow natural lake that shimmered lazily in the sun, the tall green tules at the lake's edge shoving upward like a million thin bayonets.

Kenny edged his horse over toward the tules, full of curiosity. He laughed as a big bullfrog leaped into the water with a loud and frightened splash.

Espy took deep pleasure from the boy's laugh. He had heard few of them the last couple of years.

A cowboy lounging in the shade on the shack's small front porch arose without haste as the man and the boy rode up. The puncher dropped his feet to the ground and sat up on the porch edge. He eyed the riders with lazy curiosity a minute before he spoke.

"Howdy. Git down and come in."

Espy raised his hand in greeting and swung to the ground. He heard the squeak of a bedspring inside the house. Another cowboy came to the door, sleepy-headed, his hair tousled. He was in stocking feet.

"Company," he observed. "Come on into the shade and rest yourselves. We'll have dinner in a little while, if old Dolph ever decides to leave them cattle alone and come in."

Espy told them his name, but not what he was. They showed no sign of recognition. They hadn't heard about the new manager yet. The way it looked to Espy, it was just as well.

"Hadn't really expected to find anybody around the house at this time of day," he say. "Figured you'd be out working."

Evidently they took him for someone just passing through the country.

"Why, mister," spoke the cowboy who had been lying on the porch, "this is the best outfit to work for that you ever saw. Work one hour, sleep the rest of the day if you want to. And if you've got some old hard-head like Dolph around, you can sleep the other hour too. He'll do the work."

Espy turned his attention to loosening his cinch, holding back the disgust which was beginning to rub against his grain.

"I'd like to work for an outfit like that," he said.

The other cowboy spoke up. "Then you ought to've come before Frank Bowman passed on. Tell him you were broke and needed work, and he'd put you right on.

Once you get on with the Figure 4, you just stay on. Frank Bowman never fired a man.''

"Even if he didn't work?"

"Aw," said the puncher, "we work if Sam Kirk comes over. He's the foreman. Way this house sits, we can see Sam before he can see us. Gives us time to get out and get busy.''

"What about this Dolph you mentioned?"

The cowboy laughed. "He's one of these old mossbacks who thinks the only thing a man was born for was to work. So if he wants to work, we just let him. Makes it easier on us.''

Espy felt the tingle of anger putting its splotch of color into his face. The cook, Jess Cooley, had told him there would be three men at this camp. He knew two of them who wouldn't be here much longer.

It was well past one o'clock on Espy's stem-winding pocket watch before the middle-aged puncher named Dolph came riding in wearily on a tired, sweat-streaked dun horse. On his way through the fenced horse pasture he had tossed a loop around the neck of a fresh sorrel and was leading him up to the shed at the end of his rope. This would be his afternoon mount, Espy knew.

Espy pitched in and helped the old puncher whip up a noon meal. The other two cowboys were not much help, except at eating it. After dinner Dolph saddled the sorrel and rode out again.

Anger tugging downward at the corners of his mouth, Espy said to his son, "Come on Kenny. Time we were going.''

He cast a sharp glance at the two lazy cowboys. Impulse urged him to fire them right now, right there. But judgment told him to wait. What was true here might be true at other line camps. Even the headquarters itself. He'd wait a few days, then. He'd wait until he had had a chance to observe all the men quietly, and make his own judgment. Then, when the axe did fall, he'd make it one fast, smooth stroke.

He waited even longer than he had expected. He watched, he asked careful questions, and he listened. Then one day he sent Cotton and a couple of other cowboys out to the line camps to fetch in all the men who could possibly get away.

They all hunkered under the shade of a big china-berry tree in the early afternoon sun, patiently curious. Stepping off the syndicate house porch and walking calmly down toward the tree, Espy could see the sudden surprise in some of the faces as men from the line camps realized who he was. In some of the faces he caught the sick flush of dismay.

He stopped in front of the men, still standing in the sun. He stood silently for the space of a minute or two, his eyes drifting from one man to another, catching curiosity in some faces, amusement, shame in a couple, and resentment in two or three.

At the big house, Mary Bowman stood watching. And at one edge of the group of men, barely inside the shade of the big tree, Sam Kirk waited worriedly.

"Men," Espy said, "I've met everyone who's here. And you've all met me, even if some of you didn't know who I was. I'm the new manager of the Figure 4. I haven't been here long, but I've already seen some things I liked, and lots of things I didn't like. I've seen some men who'd be a credit to any outfit they worked for. And I've seen some who aren't worth killing."

He reached in his shirt pocket. "I've got a list of names here. These men can draw their pay at the kitchen. I've already given Jess Cooley the checks. I want these men off the Figure 4 by sundown tomorrow. And I don't ever want them to come back."

He read the names, nine of them. He saw shock strike in the group, one man after another, like a hard-swing hickory singletree.

Finished with the names, he paused a moment. Sullenness had settled in some of the nine faces. One man had already arisen and was walking stiffly toward the barn, to get his horse.

"As for the rest," Espy said, "I'm pleased with most of you. There's nothing that makes a man's job better than to be able to work with good men. There are a few borderline cases here, though, some I might ought to've fired but didn't. If you're one of them, you likely know it.

"I'm giving you another chance. But I'll be watching you. From now on, any man who works for the Figure 4 will *work* for it. I don't drive men, but I want everyone to do his share, the same way I'll try to do mine. I'll expect loyalty to the ranch and full obedience to Sam Kirk and myself."

He unfolded another sheet of paper. "I've got a list of rules drawn up here, to be posted in the bunkhouse. The same kind of rules that some of the other Panhandle outfits are making. If you don't think you can live up to them, I want you to quit now."

Turning his back, he walked briskly toward the syndicate house. Mary Bowman stepped down off her porch and quartered across to intercept him. Scarlet worked in her oval face. Her slender hands were at her sides, flexing in hard anger.

"That was a little raw, don't you think? Even for a syndicate man."

"Raw? Maybe it was. But it was long overdue."

"My father hired those men."

"And *I* fired them." He tipped his hat to her and went on into his house.

Among the names he had read was that of a cowboy

named Claude Hatch. Hatch stood six feet tall in his polished, knee-high black boots. A year short of thirty, he was kid-proud of his broad, strong shoulders. He shaved every night, a highly uncommon practice among the Panhandle cowpunchers. He kept his black hair trimmed neatly, and he spent many an hour before the cracked bunkhouse mirror, combing his hair down slick and neat.

Potentially a good cowhand, the way Sam Kirk saw him. But the trouble was, the only thing he ever worked hard at was catching Mary Bowman's attention. He figured his bearing and his natural good looks ought to go right well with a pretty girl and her big, fine ranch. Sometimes, out of sight of Sam Kirk and everybody else, he sat down under the shade of a cottonwood and dreamed about it.

Mr. Claude Hatch—maybe they'd call him "Colonel"—a prominent figure anywhere he went in Texas, from Tascosa to Austin. Owner of the Figure 4, biggest ranch in the state. Sure, it'd be the biggest some day. Give him a chance. And there'd be a pretty women on his arm to charm the senators who paused in their work to come to him and ask his advice.

Far-fetched? Not for Claude Hatch. He'd won many a pleasant smile from Mary Bowman. He'd even taken her to a couple of dances. And afterward she'd taken him into the big house and brewed up a pot of coffee for him. He'd sit there and talk with her father as if he were as big a cowman as Bowman, and not just a ranch hand who in a few minutes would crawl into a hard cot in the same bunkhouse with upwards of a dozen other men.

Hatch had been biding his time. He'd dropped her a few broad hints that he had marriage on his mind, and she hadn't turned him away. That was all the sign he needed.

Now, suddenly, everything had exploded in his face.

Hatch stood helplessly, the shock draining down through him like a slow-burning acid. Then the anger began to rise, and it turned into a searing fury.

"He can't do it," Hatch declared.

A lazy kid named Choate snickered at him. Choate's name had been called too. "The hell he can't. He just did. Shine up your boots, Claude boy, and we'll head for town."

"He's not going to fire me," Hatch thundered, "not by a damn sight."

Hatch's narrowed eyes saw Mary Bowman standing on her porch. In long, angry strides he started her way.

"Mary," he said quickly, stepping hurriedly onto the porch, "you heard him call my name? You heard him fire me?"

Her voice was strained. "I heard him."

Hatch said, "You're not really going to let him do it, are you, Mary? You're going to stop him, aren't you?"

She shrugged. "I don't know how I can."

"But you're still half-owner of this ranch. He can't do something like this if you don't want him to."

Levelly she said, "You're just partly right, Claude. Yes, it's still half my ranch. But I haven't a word of say left in the way it's run. Espy Norwood is the boss here now, the only one. I don't suppose I could even ride my own horses anymore if he said no."

Incredulously Hatch said, "You can't mean that, Mary."

She nodded. "I do mean it. I'm no better now than if I had been hired to scrub floors here."

He stood silent a moment, his mind racing with a dozen wild and desperate schemes. "I won't let him do this, Mary. You know how I feel about you. You know I don't want to leave this ranch—and you."

She watched him, half in pity. She had always liked

Claude, in a way. He was pleasant company. But that was all he was, and all he was ever likely to be. Behind his handsome face and his proud smile, she knew he was empty. He was a man to dream big dreams, but he was a man who could never bring those dreams to reality.

In a way, then, she thought, it was probably best that he go. She didn't want to keep leading him on, yet she didn't want to make an outright break with him.

"I won't let him separate us, Mary," Hatch went on earnestly. "I'll run him out of the country before I'll let him do that to us."

Run him out of the country. A sudden idea set her to tingling. She measured Hatch's shoulders with her eyes. Here was a chance, a big chance.

"That might be the way," she said, covering her quick excitement. Then she cautioned. "But Norwood is no weakling. He's a stubborn man. Quirt Wolford tried to stop him and couldn't."

Hatch's shoulders squared, fists knotting. *"I'll* stop him, Mary."

A new determination driving him, he stepped down from the porch and strode down the slope toward the syndicate house. He stopped in front of it, hands on his hips. "Norwood," he called loudly, "come out here."

Espy Norwood came out onto the porch. He eyed Hatch sternly. "Your check's over at the cookshack, Hatch."

Hatch took a deep breath, swelling his broad chest. "I'm not picking up that check, Norwood. You're not man enough to fire me."

Disappointment was bitter as ashes in Espy's mouth. He had hoped this wouldn't happen. But all along, he had known it probably would. Out of nine men, at least one was bound to come looking for trouble.

Espy stared at Hatch, trying to weigh him, trying to decide how much of this was bluster and how much was fight. "I *have* fired you, Hatch."

The cowboys had begun to scatter. Now the angry lift of fight-talk started drawing them back. They gathered well behind Claude Hatch, none of them taking a hand, but all of them watching. Hatch looked back and saw them, and their presence strengthened his determination.

"And I say I'm not going, Norwood. Come down off that porch. Come down and I'll show you whether you can fire me or not."

Espy drew a long, deep breath, regret lying heavily within him. He'd have to make his work good now. Back up, and he'd lose control of this ranch.

Kenny edged worriedly out onto the porch. Espy glanced at him, then back to Hatch. "Go back in the house, son," he said quietly to the boy.

He walked down the steps and out toward Hatch. Two paces from the tall cowboy, he stopped. He set his feet solidly, his weight hard upon his heels.

The flare in Hatch's eyes betrayed him before he stepped forward and lashed out with his fist. Espy ducked back just enough, then caught Hatch in the stomach with a quick, hard punch. A gust of breath tore from the cowboy. He doubled, caught himself, and launched a smashing right that struck Espy's shoulder, spinning him back.

Regaining balance, Espy crouched defensively. Hatch rushed him, fists closed. He was a different kind of fighter from Quirt Wolford. He was a show fighter, a man who considered himself a boxer.

Espy struck at him and missed. Hatch's fist stabbed forward while his left stayed in close to his face, covering himself. Espy caught part of the blow on his chin.

He staggered, while two or three of the fired cowboys yipped in glee and urged Hatch on. Hatch came in punching.

Espy warded off the blows. A hard anger began to rise as his tongue caught the warm salt taste of blood on his lips. Deliberately he stepped closer, almost chin to chin, taking two body blows in return for a chance to bring up a savage uppercut at Hatch's jaw.

Hatch reeled, his hands flying up to cover his face. Jaw ridged, Espy dealt him a breath-jarring blow to the ribs, and another to Hatch's stomach.

Blood fury exploded in Hatch's eyes. He flung away his technique, his caution. He waded in, fists driving like pump handles. Espy almost went down under their bludgeoning attack. But he caught himself and held. He went after the weak spots, the spots that Hatch was leaving uncovered in his blind rage. Striking at these, he wore the cowboy down.

Fatigue dragged on Espy's arms like sacks of lead. But he knew now that he had the fight won. He methodically forced Hatch back, putting his whole body behind the blows that became weaker and weaker, until Espy felt he could swing his arms no more.

But just when Espy was ready to fall exhausted on the steps of his house, Hatch went down and stayed down. He lay twisted, half on his side, half on his stomach. Espy swayed, then dropped weakly upon the steps, his breath labored and slow.

The watching cowboys had made no move to join in the fight. Through burning eyes. Espy watched them, wondering which way they would lean. Then two of the fired punchers stepped forward, violence in their eyes. Espy sat still, helpless to stand and defend himself.

Cotton Dulaney took several long strides and stopped in front of Espy, his fists clenched. "The boss man's give out," he said. "And if anybody thinks they can take advantage of him now, they'll have to whip me first."

The two cowboys stared menacingly at the kid, pondering whether or not to jump him. When it appeared that they would, old Jess Cooley stepped up beside the kid, his gnarled hand tight on a long chunk of stovewood.

"You're nuttier than fruitcake, button," he said quietly. "But you got the right idea. Any of them jumps you, he'll have to jump me too."

Espy could see the scales begin to tip. The other cowboys began to crowd closer. Most of them were backing up Cotton and the cook. The two fired cowhands sensed it, and the fight drained out of them.

Espy Norwood had regained enough breath that he could speak. He pushed to his feet. "The fight's over. Jess, you go on back to the cookshack, and pay off the men I told you to. Cotton, you go on about your business. The rest of you men too."

To the two cowboys who had moved to fight him, he said, "Hatch'll need help. Take him down to the bunkhouse. When he's able, you'd better travel."

The cowboys grudgingly helped the bloody-faced Hatch to his feet. Once standing, he angrily shoved them aside and stood swaying, alone. He tried to fasten his swollen eyes upon Espy. Hatred roiled in them like red-hot tar in a bucket.

"You haven't whipped me, Norwood, not by a gutful. I'll mark this up as a debt I owe you. And by God, I'll pay it, Norwood. With interest."

He staggered off toward the bunkhouse. One of the cowboys tried to help him. Hatch shoved him away and went it alone, the color boiling in his bruised and bloody face.

He turned once and shouted, "I'll be back, Norwood, you watch. I'll be back."

Espy said nothing, hoping this was the end of it but knowing it wouldn't be.

On the porch of the big house, Mary Bowman also watched, her face drained of color. Without her realizing it, her right hand gripped tensely the lace on her blouse. She watched Claude Hatch go, and she wished she hadn't urged him on.

If it hadn't been for me, she was thinking, he wouldn't have done it. But I pushed him, and now it's gone too far. There can't be any backing up.

The cords in her slender throat went tight with anxiety and with shame. Suddenly she was worry for Hatch, and sorry for Espy Norwood too.

"What have I done?" The question kept driving at her stricken mind. "I've started something and now I can't stop it. Oh, Dad, I wish you were were. I wish you could tell me what to do."

XI

Espy Norwood sat at Jess Cooley's long dining table, sipping fire-hot black coffee and studying Sam Kirk across the table. Kirk fingered a steaming cup, his eyes following the movements of the ranch cook as Cooley prepared supper.

"Yep," Kirk was saying, "I was as surprised as the rest of them. But I'll admit that you did a first-class job of culling. They're the same ones I'd've gotten rid of, if I'd thought Mary would stand for it."

"Why wouldn't she have stood for it?"

"Sentiment, mostly. Her dad hired them. She wouldn't fire them."

Espy rubbed his sore jaw, flinching as his rough hand grated across a mean bruise. "From all accounts, Frank Bowman was a good ranchman, Sam. Then how did he let himself get saddled down with all this deadwood? There's plenty of *good* cowboys needing work."

Sam shook his head. "Trouble with Mr. Frank was that he had too soft a heart. Let somebody come to him broke, down-and-out, and Mr. Frank would give him a job whether he needed him or not. And once a man got on with Mr. Frank, he had a job as long as he wanted to stay. I don't reckon Mary's dad ever fired a man in his life."

Espy came close to smiling. "He must've been a good man, Sam. I wish I could've come along soon enough to get to know him."

Kirk looked at the tabletop, memory misting his eyes a moment. "They've just about lost the mold nowadays."

Then he changed the subject. "We're going to need some men. This has left us mighty short-handed."

Espy nodded. "I thought about that even before I called in the men. I'll get some new hands, Sam. I think I know how to get some good ones."

He was thinking of Arch McCavitt. Arch was in a position to know most of the cowboys in the country. He would know which ones could be hired, and he'd know the good ones.

"I'll go to Mobeetie in a couple of days," he said. He knew the soreness from the fight would settle its full weight upon him by tomorrow. He'd wait until it waned. "We can make out a little longer."

Kenny Norwood knew the awful pangs of loneliness as he stood in front of the barn in the rosy glow of dawn and watched his father ride off toward Mobeetie. He wouldn't be back until tomorrow night, he had told Kenny.

"You go play with Joe Kirk," Espy had told him. "He can teach you lots of things."

Joe had, all right. He had taught Kenny not to stand too close to a water trough. Fellow was apt to get pushed into it. Kenny had.

He had taught Kenny a couple of wrestling holds, too, painful holds that had brought the rush of angry, helpless tears to Kenny's eyes.

Stand and fight him! That was what the chorus of outraged voices within Kenny had roared every time Joe started to run another whizzer on him. But something had kept holding Kenny back. Not fear, exactly. He'd gotten over most of his real fear of Joe Kirk. But

even yet, he knew a dull dread of physical combat.
Aunt Margaret had drilled that into him too deeply for
him to forget it easily.

Kenny watched his father ride away, and he wished
he could have gone with him. He had thought he could
never like his father again. But now Kenny found
himself listening for Espy's footsteps with a quick thrill
of gladness. He took a deep pleasure in the way Espy's
voice always went quiet for him, and the way Espy's
eyes softened as they dwelt upon his son. Kenny's heart
stirred with pride at the confident way his father went
about doing the things that had to be done.

Most especially had he swelled with pride when
Cotton Dulaney had come to the syndicate house after
Hatch and the fired riders had gone. Cotton had stood
uncertainly, looking at the floor, trying to say what was
on his mind without making it sound like soft soap.

"The boys asked me to speak for them, Mr. Norwood," Cotton said. "We all talked it over, and we
want you to know we'll back up anything you say, a
hundred per cent."

Kenny hadn't missed the happy glow in Espy's eyes.

This morning Cotton had roped out the best horse in
the company mount and turned him over to Espy.
"This here is old Baldy," he had said. "You need a
good horse, and this is him."

Four other cowboys had then done likewise. And
now Espy had a first-rate mount of company horses.
Kenny had sensed that Espy couldn't be prouder of
them if he had bought them all for five hundred dollars
apiece.

Shortly after Espy left, the cowboys began to rope
out their horses and scatter for work. Kenny watched
them, his eyes dwelling mostly upon cocky young Joe
Kirk.

Aunt Margaret had preached to him against envy, but he could not resist the envy which burned in him now. He had seen the way the cowboys kidded Joe, joshing him around, pranking him, treating him like an equal with the men. They didn't do that for Kenny. They were polite, but that was all. Even with a crowd of cowboys around him, Kenny felt alone, hopelessly alone. Maybe if he had spent his life out here, like Joe had, instead of living in the city . . .

Joe Kirk saddled his own horse and mounted him without a footlift from anybody. He rode out with three cowboys to make a hand just as if he were a grown man. Kenny knew that, and the envy burned deeper.

Joe's eyes lit upon Kenny, and mischief flickered devilishly in them. Shaking down the rope from his saddle horn, he kneed his horse toward Kenny. ''Run, calf, run!'' he shouted.

Kenny's heart leaped. Joe was going to ride him down! He turned and ran for the safety of the fence. He heard the swish of Joe's rope. The loop jerked tight around Kenny's feet and yanked them out from under him. He sprawled face down in the sand. His cheeks were burning hot as Joe's taunting laughter reached him.

He got to his feet and kicked the rope off, his teeth clenched tight. Laughing, Joe coiled his rope and rode off after the cowboys. Kenny choked with shame as he heard one of the cowboys chiding Joe. ''You oughtn't to treat the city boy that way. Not his fault he don't know nothing. They just don't teach them in the city.''

It hadn't been meant for Kenny's ears. But it had reached them just the same. His blood ran hot. He couldn't let this go on much longer.

He turned back toward the cookshack. He stopped short as he discovered old Jess Cooley standing in the doorway, watching. Jess had seen it all. Shame touched Kenny again. He'd rather anyone had seen it than Jess. Jess or his father.

Jess was diplomat enough not to mention the incident. Not directly, anyway.

"How about some cold biscuits and some fruit, cowboy?" Jess asked him in a friendly voice.

With nowhere else to go, Kenny followed the cook into the kitchen. Cooley set down a bowl with a remnant of stewed apricots in it.

"Eat them up. I need the bowl, and them apricots is too good to feed to the chickens."

Eating them, Kenny lost his anger. He watched Cooley bring down a huge crock jar off a shelf, check it, and shove it back. Rising sourdough swelled up over the top of it, dough that soon would be biscuits on the table. Cooley started mixing up another batch of dough for a second jar that he had emptied in making biscuits. Kenny watched, fascinated, while Cooley punched dough into the jar. It was far short of the top.

"Aren't you going to fill it up?" he asked.

Cooley shook his head. "It'll rise like that other one yonder. Put any more dough in it and it'd get all over the kitchen."

Kenny's mouth was wide open. "Gosh."

He squirmed a minute, wanting to ask a question and hoping it wouldn't sound too foolish. "Say, Jess, what do you do to make it swell up that way?"

Furtively Jess looked all around him as if making sure there weren't any cowboys around to hear. Then he leaned close to Kenny's ear and whispered:

"I wouldn't want them finicky cowpunchers to find out my secret. You won't tell anybody."

"I won't tell."

"Well," the cook said cautiously, "I keep two big

old bullfrogs in the bottom of each of them jars. They puff up the dough for me.''

Kenny's mouth dropped wider open. "Gosh!"

Then doubt crowded in, and he grinned uncertainly. "Aw, Jess, you're just loading me. That's not the truth.''

Cooley went on kneading the dough, snaggle teeth showing in his broad grin. "Well, son," he said shortly, "I reckon I *was* pulling your leg a little. Truth of the matter is, I only got *one* frog in each of them crocks.''

Cooley waited awhile before he brought up the touchy subject. "Joe Kirk's thrown a booger into you, hasn't he, kid?''

Hotly Kenny said, "I'm not scared of him.''

Cooley frowned, not making any comment.

Deeply disturbed, Kenny asked, "What's the matter with Joe? I try to get along with him, honest I do. But every time I try to make friends with him he pulls something on me. Has he always been this mean?''

The cook said patiently, "He's not mean, Kenny. Oh, he's got more mischief in him than a dozen pet coons, but he's not mean. It's just that ever since he's been big enough to wean, cowboys have been hoorawing him. Cowboys will always bedevil a kid.

"Now you've come along. This is the first time he's ever had a chance to bedevil anybody else the way they've done him. And he's gone clear off the deep end with it.''

"What can I do, Jess?''

"Well, sir, the Book says that if a man smites you on one cheek, you're supposed to turn him the other one. Now it looks to me like you've run plumb out of cheeks. So, it's about time to beat the everlasting whey out of him.''

Kenny looked away, distaste wrinkling up his nose.

This wasn't the first time he'd considered that possibility. He'd thought about it a lot.

"Maybe I could do it, Jess. I don't know. But I don't want to fight him. I hate to fight."

The cook's eyes were sympathetic. "Sure, son. Most people hate to fight. But sometimes there's no other way out. Look at your daddy now. You don't think he wanted to fight Quirt Wolford, do you? But he had to. It was either that or run. And he's no man for running. He didn't want to fight Claude Hatch, either. You could see that in his face. He hated it. But he had to fight or quit, and he's no quitter.

"You're in the same place, kid. It's either fight or keep on running. And I'm going to be mighty disappointed in you if you run. Mighty disappointed."

With that, Cooley hushed up, his face grave. Kenny's pulse quickened. He felt the blood begin rushing to his face. This was an ultimatum. Either he stood his ground now, or Jess was through with him.

Kenny walked outside, his hands suddenly cold and sweaty, and a million needles prickling the seat of his pants.

All morning long he paced around the barn, his mind running away with him in countless wild daydreams of vicious combat. He was a gladiator, his huge iron sword slashing Joe to the ground while the Romans cheered. He was an armored knight of King Arthur, his heavy lance sending the evil knight, Joe, spinning from his saddle. He was a marshal in Dodge City, blasting outlaw Joe full of holes with the two six-guns he wore at his sides.

And then Joe came riding in alone, ahead of the cowboys, and he was plain Kenny Norwood again, his heart thumping like that of a caught rabbit. Kenny watched Joe, near-panic surging in him. Not now, a weak voice cried within him. Another time, not now.

But in the doorway of the cookshack, Jess Cooley stood with arms folded, waiting.

It *had* to be now.

How was he to do it? He knew he couldn't bring himself to start a fight. Once it started, he might be all right. But to start it himself . . .

Watching Joe, he almost backed into the water trough. The water trough! That's what would swing it.

Pulse hammering, he waited beside the trough, trying to act as if he didn't see Joe coming. He heard Joe swing down, heard the slap of leather as the youngster tied his bridle reins to the fence. There was a moment of hesitation. Then Joe was moving toward him, footsteps almost silent in the sand.

Tensely Kenny watched Joe's shadow. Not long before noon, the shadow was a short one. But Kenny saw it, and he saw it suddenly move forward as Joe lunged to push Kenny into the trough.

Kenny stepped aside. He grabbed Joe's shoulder and gave the startled boy a hard shove, straight into the trough. Face down, Joe floundered and gasped and choked. Then he came up, spouting water, his clothes soaked. Eyes raging, he rushed at Kenny, swinging his fists wildly. He hit Kenny twice.

Then Kenny hit him, right on the nose. And suddenly all Kenny's fear was gone. He'd started now, and he was mad, mad clear through. He thrust aside all the restraint that Aunt Margaret had drilled into him. He was going to finish this thing, right here and right now.

Everything he had, he put behind his tight-clenched fists. He drove them into Joe like the kick of a mule. His fury crackled and burned in him like brush afire. Joe was hitting him, too, but he hardly felt the blows. Desperation driving him, he kept pounding, forcing Joe back, and back, and back.

Sobbing in pain and anger, the surprised Joe Kirk

gave ground until at least he stood with his back against a picket shed. Kenny's arms were tired and heavy, but he went on with it. At last Joe slid down, and lay on his back in the sand.

Kenny dropped to his knees, astraddle Joe Kirk. Bloody-nosed and bruised, Joe was choked, half crying, his weak hands fighting futilely to hold back Kenny's tight fists.

Kenny stopped hitting him. With both hands he grabbed Joe's hair and started beating the boy's head against the side of the shed. Joe cried for him to stop.

"Holler 'calf rope,' " Kenny demanded.

Joe was a little slow about it. Kenny bumped his head some more. Tears streaming down his sand-crusted cheeks, Joe finally gave in.

"Calf rope," he cried weakly.

Kenny stood up, knees wobbly. He leaned on the shed for support. For the first time he saw Jess Cooley standing there watching, the edges of his droopy mustache trying hard to lift in a grin.

Cooley reached down and helped Joe to a stand. Sniffling, Joe took one weak swing at Kenny, missed him, and stepped back quickly to keep from being hit in return.

"Now, Joe," Cooley said, "it looks to me like you've had about enough."

With his big hand he tried to wipe off some of the sand which had clung to Joe's wet clothing. It was useless.

The cook said, "You've done your hoorawing and gotten your comeuppance for it. From now on, you'll know better than to pick at Kenny Norwood."

Joe didn't answer. He sniffled, his eyes misty, his face still flushed with rage.

"Now then," Cooley went on, "Kenny wants to be

friends with you. He's tried ever since he's been here.
Why don't you shake hands with him?''

Stubbornly Joe put his hands behind him.

Cooley frowned darkly. ''There's nobody seen this
but me. You want me to tell the cowboys how bad this
town kid whipped you?''

That brought a quick alarm to Joe's freckled face.

''Then you go on and shake hands. And if you don't
make friends with Kenny, I'll tell the cowboys everything. I'll even tell them you cried and hollered 'calf
rope.' ''

With great reluctance, Joe Kirk brought his right
hand forward. Kenny's own hand was beginning to
hurt, his knuckles torn and bruised. But he shook Joe's
hand and grinned.

Cooley smiled. ''That's better. Now, Joe, you get
back in that water trough and wash the sand off of you,
and the blood. You can tell your mother your horse
threw you in it. If she asks me, I'll tell her the same
thing.''

Joe crawled back into the trough and began rinsing
off the sand. The water seemed to cool his temper. Out
of the trough, he pulled off his clothes and wrung them
out. Kenny helped him.

''Joe,'' Kenny experimented in a friendly voice,
''I've watched you riding calves. I wonder if you could
teach me?''

Joe grunted. ''I doubt it.''

''I bet you could. You're an awfully good rider.''

The unexpected compliment got to Joe where he
lived. After a time he said, ''You really think so?
Honest Injun?''

''Sure.''

Joe rubbed his aching jaw. His resistance melted. He
started to grin. ''All right, Kenny, I'll teach you. Only

you better not bawl when the big ones throw you off.''

A bruise was beginning to darken around one of Kenny's eyes. But both eyes were shining like silver dollars.

"I won't bawl, Joe, you'll see. I won't bawl."

XII

GID BOWMAN saw that Claude Hatch's glass was nearly empty. He reached across the table and filled it from his bottle. And on second thought, he filled his own as well. Hatch had taken care of the better part of the bottle already. Now he hunched in his chair in Arch McCavitt's Mobeetie saloon, his eyes swollen, his face florid, from too much whisky.

Bowman dipped the chewing end of his cigar into his glass, then shoved it into his mouth. He hadn't allowed himself to take too much today. He had business to attend to. "So Norwood just flat run you off, did he?" he prodded Hatch.

"Not for good, he didn't," Hatch declared. He spoke with a little difficulty, his tongue thick. "Mary won't stand for it."

"I guess she will," Bowman commented. "She could've stopped him if she'd really wanted to."

Hatch leaned forward heatedly, his face threateningly close. "I tell you, there wasn't anything she could do about it."

Bowman frowned, biting hard on his cigar and drawing back from Hatch's anger. "You don't really believe that, do you, Claude? If she'd demanded that Norwood keep you, he'd've done it. But she didn't. And you know why? I think Norwood's stealing her from you, boy."

Hatch jumped up, his hands grabbing for Bowman's collar. Bowman leaned backward. Dizziness caught Hatch and made him slump into his chair again. He knotted his fists, but he couldn't bring his eyes to meet Bowman's.

A flicker of a smile tugged at Bowman's mouth, and he covered it. Why, he'd soon have this hollow-headed kid eating out of his hand.

"See there, boy," Bowman said, "you knew it too. You just wouldn't admit it to yourself. That sneaking syndicate man is taking Mary over, just like he's taken over the ranch."

Face sick, Hatch rubbed his shaky hands, hard. "I'll kill him, Gid."

Bowman shook his head. "They'd just hang you, and what good would it do you then? Naw, Claude, that's not the way to settle up with Norwood."

"What would *you* do?" Hatch asked in misery.

"You really want to even up with him?"

Hatch nodded. "Anything I can do."

Bowman leaned forward to speak, then settled back and waited. Arch McCavitt was walking his way. From what Bowman had heard, McCavitt was some kind of old *compadre* of Norwood's.

When McCavitt had gone on past, Bowman said quietly, "You just come along with me, Claude. We got plans for our friend Norwood. And you can help. We can use a good levelheaded man like you."

Hatch half snickered. "You? You can't do anything but drink whisky."

Bowman's lips flattened a moment, red spurting into his face. Then he caught himself. "It's not just me, Claude. Quirt Wolford is in on it, too. Don't you think Quirt Wolford will know what to do about Norwood?"

Hatch stared, surprised. "Wolford? Yeah, I reckon he would."

Bowman stood up, smiling thinly. "Well, then, come on along with me, Claude. We'll start out for my camp tonight. Tomorrow we'll see Quirt."

He helped Hatch to his feet. He slipped Hatch's arm over his shoulder to give the drunken cowboy support. Hatch was near collapse. It was hard work for Bowman, half-carrying and half-dragging Hatch toward the door.

Bowman stopped cold as a man walked in and stood before the door, letting his eyes accustom themselves to the dimmer light. Espy Norwood!

Bowman and Norwood quietly eyed each other a moment. Bowman was the first to speak. "Howdy, Norwood."

Norwood answered him with a short and simple "Howdy," his eyes on Hatch.

Bowman said, "Just helping the boy out, Norwood. Some fellers never do know when they've had enough."

Espy watched the two men labor out the wide door and into the sandy street. Then he turned toward the bar, worried. What in the dickens was Gid Bowman doing with Claude Hatch?

He shrugged, shoving the question aside as red-haired Arch McCavitt came from behind the bar, his hand outstretched. "Have they chased you off already?" Arch grinned, knowing better. "I hear they've tried."

Sitting at a table with McCavitt, Espy told what all had happened. McCavitt nodded quietly. He'd heard most of it.

Espy said, "So we need some new hands, Arch. I hoped you could help me find some."

Mischief played in Arch's eyes. "Maybe I can. I'll find you some men just as good as I am."

Espy grinned. "That's what I'm afraid of. You'll have to do a right smart better than that."

He headed back toward the ranch the next morning, confident in Arch's promise to help.

"It may take a few days," Arch had said, "but I'll find you some men. I'll send them out as they get ready."

Espy had asked Arch something else. "Do you know who usually takes count for the Figure 4 when it's on roundup?"

Arch's eyebrows had lifted, "Why?"

"Just curious. Wanted to do a little checking."

Bowman's tally books had continued to worry him, even though they had been exactly the same as those the colonel had, and balanced out letter-perfect. Espy still hadn't been able to shake off the doubt which Cotton Dulaney had started in him.

He'd seen Arch's obvious reluctance in answering and had wondered about it. "Well," Arch said, "I went out to the Figure 4 camp a couple of times this spring. The counters were Sam Kirk and old Charlie Burnside."

Espy hadn't heard the name before.

"Charlie's an old bachelor," Arch explained. "Got him a little ranch out yonder toward the Figure 4, a little to the north. Good stockman, and the best hand at counting cattle you ever saw. Frank Bowman always liked to use him. Besides, Charlie generally needed a little extra money."

Riding out of Mobeetie under the rosy light of sunup. Espy bore a little north of the Figure 4. By noon he reached Charlie Burnside's camp. An old man stood beside the open door of a dugout, where woodsmoke curled upward from a crooked chimney in the sod roof. The prairie wind played through his long gray whiskers.

"Git down," the old man greeted him openhandedly. "Git down and come in. Chuck'll be ready pretty soon now."

Espy introduced himself. Burnside pumped his

hand. Age had weakened the old ranchman's grip, but it hadn't dimmed his smile.

"Sure am pleased to meet you. Hadn't heard they'd gotten them a new manager over there yet. Just figured Mary was going to handle it."

Espy didn't know what answer to give to that, so he gave none. The old man added, "We don't hear much, just me and old Ramon on this place by ourselves. Ain't often either one of us gits to town."

Espy didn't ask him about the cattle counts until the two of them and Burnside's Mexican helper had finished eating. Espy and the old ranchman sat in the shade of a brush arbor that had been built beside the dugout to substitute for a porch.

Holding a tight rein on his eagerness, Espy asked. "They tell me you helped count the Figure 4 stock during the spring roundup." He made it sound almost as if he wasn't really interested—just making conversation.

"That I did, that I did. Been doing it for three or four years now." He added with a bit of pride, "May not be good for much else anymore, but I'm still the best cattle counter hereabouts."

Espy's hand was nervously flexing, open and shut, open and shut, "Would you remember what those counts were?"

The old man studied a moment, his eyes fixed on the broad horizon, where not a single tree broke the gentle swell of the prairie. "Well, sir, I couldn't rightly say anymore. I handed all the tally books over to Sam Kirk, for Frank Bowman. Frank's health was failing him last spring. He didn't get out to the roundup much."

Espy's eyes sharpened. "You mean he gave Sam Kirk full authority?"

Burnside nodded. "Sure. Sam always was Frank

Bowman's right-hand man. There never was a better foreman. He'd've made the syndicate a good manager, if they'd had sense enough to hire him.''

The old man reddened a little then. ''No offense meant, Norwood. I judge you to be a pretty good cowman yourself.''

''Thanks.''

Espy frowned, a growing knot of suspicion tightening in him. ''I wonder why they didn't keep your tally books?''

Burnside shrugged. ''Sam always took count same as I did. I reckon he checked my books against his, then turned his own in to Mr. Frank. Chances are he just threw mine away. No sense in keeping two sets anyhow.''

A tingle of excitement began to work through Espy. Here at last was something to put his finger on.

''Have the cattle numbers gone down much since you've been helping the Figure 4?''

Burnside nodded. ''A right smart. You can probably find that in Mr. Frank's books.'' No use telling the old man it *didn't* show on Mr. Frank's books.

Espy pressed, ''Taking the south end of the ranch for example, how much would you say the cattle have been cut down?''

''Down there, I reckon they've been trimmed way more than half in the last couple of years. Over the rest of the ranch, a little less. Seems to me like I remember the tally down on the lower end, what Mr. Frank always called the south ranch. There was something over a thousand head, maybe twelve hundred, last branding. Used to be a sight more than that. One year we worked three thousand head on the south ranch.''

Anger filled Espy's eyes. Twelve hundred head. Yet the tally books showed twenty-seven hundred. He remembered that.

And Sam Kirk had handled the books!

A slow-burning anger ate at Espy all the way back to the Figure 4 headquarters. He knew a vague disappointment, too. He'd liked Sam Kirk. He had seen readily enough that Sam was a first-class stockman. And Frank Bowman evidently had trusted Sam through the years. But this business about the tally books was going to be hard to explain.

Espy rode in above the barns. Boyish laughter reached out to him long before he got there. The high-spirited shouting of youngsters led him around the back side of the barn.

In a pole corral Joe Kirk had snubbed a big bawling calf to a post. Kenny Norwood sat astradle the struggling calf while Joe drew a rope tight around the calf's belly and over Kenny's hands.

"Ready," Kenny said, and Joe turned the calf loose.

Bawling, the calf bucked and plunged. Kenny bounced from one side to the other, laughing at the top of his voice. Then he lost balance and began to slip low off one side. He hung precariously there for two jumps, then sailed off and rolled in the sand.

Joe Kirk ran to him and helped him up. "You're doing better, Tex. You rode him six jumps that time. I counted them."

Grinning, Kenny wiped the sand from his face. It was a bruised face, and there was a big black ring around one eye. "Six jumps? Did I, really?"

"You sure 'nuff did. Want to give her another whirl?"

"You bet your boots."

They saw Espy sitting his horse, watching them. Kenny walked hurriedly to the fence. His exuberance spilled forth in a flood of words. "Hello, Daddy. I'm learning to ride calves. I'm doing pretty good, too, because Joe says so himself. And you know what else? He calls me Tex.''

Espy's throat was tight, but he managed a smile. He hadn't heard Kenny laughing like that since he was a tiny boy. And Kenny hadn't looked at Espy this way in years.

Espy's eyes stung him, and he blinked hard. This durned sand . . .

Turning his horse loose, Espy walked up the slope toward Sam Kirk's house. Sam sat on the front porch, braiding a set of rawhide bridle reins. Sam nodded at Espy, then rolled the reins even under the weight of his boot. ''Find us some men?'' he asked.

Espy nodded, his mouth tight. ''We'll get the men. Found something else, too. I want to talk to you, Sam. Is Helen in the house?''

Sam shook his head, curious. ''No, she's out back, watering her flower beds.''

''Good,'' Espy said. ''No use for her to hear this.''

Espy's hands were nervous. He rubbed them along the seams of his pants. ''I want you to answer me straight, Sam. Did you turn in a true set of tallies to Frank Bowman after the spring roundup?''

Sudden harshness rushed to Kirk's brown face. ''What do you mean by that?''

''Just what I asked you. Did you? Or were those tallies doctored up?''

Sam Kirk moved to his feet. He stepped down off the porch to the same level as Espy Norwood. His nostrils flared. ''Nobody's ever called me a crook, Norwood.''

Espy stared levelly into Kirk's brittle-turned eyes. ''And *I* don't want to. But I had a talk with Charlie Burnside. What he told me doesn't check out with the tally books you turned in to Frank Bowman.''

''What did he tell you?''

"He said he counted only about twelve hundred head on the south ranch. Tally books place the count close to twenty-seven hundred. You turned those figures in, Sam. I want to know why they're wrong."

Espy could see the pulse beating in Sam Kirk's throat. Kirk's chin was high and steady. "Charlie Burnside is wrong."

"He's got a reputation as a top counter."

"As a counter, yes. But he's got the poorest memory in the state of Texas. If he doesn't write a count down in a hurry, he forgets it. He probably can't tell you how old he is without looking it up."

For a moment Espy weakened under a serious doubt. What if the old man *was* wrong?

But he knew within reason that Burnside couldn't be that far wrong. The fault lay elsewhere. And it could only be in Sam Kirk.

"That all you've got to say, Sam?"

Kirk nodded. "That's all there is to say."

Stiffly Sam Kirk stood and watched as Espy strode off toward his house. Sam's jaw was ridged, his face red. Then his hands began to tremble. His shoulders slumped as he climbed the steps to the porch. He stopped abruptly.

Helen stood just inside the door, her face drained white. "Sam!" she breathed. "Sam, what's wrong? What's this all about?"

It was a moment before he answered her. "It was nothing, Helen. I wish you hadn't heard it."

She stepped out onto the porch. Her right hand gripped his arm. "Sam, there *is* something wrong. I can see it in your face. Maybe if you'd tell me, I could help."

He shook his head emphatically. "I said there's nothing to tell."

Before she could speak again, he turned quickly, stepped down off the porch, and headed for the barn in long, stiff strides.

Helen Kirk clutched one of the porch posts, watching him until he was out of sight. Her eyes glistened, near tears. She hesitated, trying to make up her mind. Then she stepped down off the porch and hurried toward Norwood's house.

Espy looked up in surprise as she came in. "Helen." One look at her, and he knew she had heard.

Her hands were clasped fearfully against her breast. "Espy," she said, "what is it? What has Sam done?"

Espy almost wished he'd never come to the Figure 4. He felt his heart tighten. He waited a moment, mustering up courage. "I'm not sure just what all he's done, Helen. But I do know that the spring tallies are false, and that he wrote them. The rest of it, you'll have to guess, just the way I'm guessing."

Helen looked at him with stricken eyes. A sob welled up in her throat. "Oh, Espy, Espy, what can I do for him?" she cried.

Espy's throat swelled. He did not answer, for he knew no answer to give.

XIII

THE PROCESSION strung out for three hundred yards, twenty horses and four riders. In an easy, jogging trot, they followed an old wagon trail, two narrow ruts worn into the prairie sod, two ruts that were the only visible break in a great swelling, rolling ocean of short grass stretching to the horizon and far beyond.

A long-legged, loose-gaited *grulla* gelding was out in the lead, setting the pace, his head held high and proud. They were headed for the south camp of the Figure 4. The big *grulla* had spent much of his life there, and the homing instinct was strong in him. The other horses followed along, each in the place into which he had settled. Younger horses earlier in the morning had tried to take the lead, but the cantankerous *grulla* wasn't having it. With his ears backed down and his sharp teeth seeking blood, he had put them all in their place.

Espy Norwood and Sam Kirk followed a little way behind the loose horses. They had ridden almost stirrup to stirrup since shortly after daylight. Now it was two hours short of noon, and hardly a dozen words had passed from one man to the other. The tight barrier of silence between them was almost as solid as an adobe wall.

Far back, bringing up the rear, Kenny Norwood and freckled-faced Joe Kirk laughed and talked and played. For an hour one had been a Comanche Indian and the

other an Indian fighter. A curt warning from Sam Kirk
to Joe finally had ended that game.

The boys had dropped back, slowing their horses to a
walk. They let their fathers get three hundred yards
ahead of them. Then, yelling like two wild Indians,
they raked spurs along their horses' sides and plunged
into a breakneck race.

Over his shoulder, Espy watched the two youngsters
thundering down upon him. His face relaxed momentarily, and a grin played at the corners of his mouth.

Joe pulled his horse to a sudden, sliding stop, the
dust swirling past him. He looked back proudly at the
two parallel marks the sharp hind hoofs had cut into the
ground.

Sam Kirk twisted half around in the saddle, his eyes
impatient. "Joe, if you buttons don't quit running those
horses like that, you'll both be afoot before we get to
the south camp."

Joe said, "All right, Papa." And in three minutes he
would forget again.

Espy gave Kenny a sharp, reproving glance. But
inwardly he was smiling. Kenny's happy laughter had
been like music to him. He had spent hours puzzling
about the change which had come to Kenny. He didn't
rightly know the reason, and Kenny wasn't talking.
One thing sure, Espy was proud of that boy.

They rode another mile, working into the rougher
ground. Behind him Espy could hear the earnest talk
and the high-lifting laughter of the youngsters.

At last he broke the long silence between himself and
Sam Kirk. "We haven't run across many cattle the last
few miles," he pointed out.

Kirk made no immediate answer. It had been the
better part of a week now since Espy had ridden in from
Charlie Burnside's ranch and demanded an explanation

about the tallies. He still hadn't gotten one that satisfied him.

Presently Kirk said, "You still don't believe me, do you?"

Espy didn't answer. Kirk added, "They don't value a man's word the way they used to."

Bluntly Espy replied, "Sometimes a man's word doesn't carry the value that it used to."

The fury in Kirk's eyes leaped at Espy. Then Kirk touched spurs to his mount and circled around to the side of the long string of horses. There he stayed, nursing his anger.

Espy asked himself for the twentieth time why he hadn't fired Sam Kirk the day he rode in from Burnside's. But he knew. It was Kenny, and reckless young Joe Kirk. And perhaps most of all, it was warm-eyed Helen Kirk.

There was one answer. A roundup, and a full count. But a roundup took time, and there wouldn't be enough before the lawyer Slagel arrived with the syndicate directors, dead set on wrecking the colonel.

And even if he did prove the number short, would that help the colonel? No, chances were it would hurt, and hurt bad.

Deeply troubled, he rode with his gaze on the ground.

Ahead, the trail pitched abruptly into broken ground, into a brush-lined draw where a downpour of rain would sometimes bring a violent rush of mud-red floodwater that could sweep a whole herd of cattle away.

The horses bunched up closer as they slanted off into the draw. Sam Kirk yelled at the drags. Espy heard the two boys riding just behind him as he started down the slope.

He saw the two horsemen almost as quickly as they saw him. Two horsemen, working down along the fringe of the brush, pushing a small bunch of cattle ahead of them. Cattle with the Figure 4 brand. And these weren't Figure 4 men.

For a long moment, surprise was the master of all the men. Then the rustlers' hands streaked upward, and fire belched from their guns.

Espy's first thought was of the boys behind him. He turned and yelled for them to get away.

Terror swept through the loose horses. They stampeded, breaking away from the thunder of the guns. Their panic seized Kenny's horse. He bolted, racing along the edge of the brush. Kenny tried to hold him, but the horse had cold-jawed. Then it was all Kenny could do to hold tight to the saddle horn and try to duck the heavy branches that plucked at him.

Espy's horse panicked, dropping his head and beginning to buck. Espy struggled to hold the mount's head up. And all the time Espy's eyes were on the helpless boy, his heart high in his throat.

He managed somehow to get the horse straightened out and to spur off after Kenny. But by that time Sam Kirk was ahead of him, sinking spurs into his horse's ribs.

Espy saw the heavy branch hit Kenny and knock him spinning fom the saddle. But Kenny didn't fall clear. Espy heard a sharp cry of despair and knew it was his own voice. Kenny's foot was hung in the stirrup!

"Kenny!" Espy cried out again, but his voice was lost in the rush of the wind. He spurred harder, but he saw the lift of dust as the boy's head and shoulders struck the ground. The heart and hope went out of Espy. He was too far behind. He could never save his boy now.

But Sam Kirk was not too far behind. Spurring hard, he closed the gap. Then his strong hand closed on the trailing bridle reins. He took a quick wrap around his saddle horn and eased the scared horse down to a trot, then to a walk, careful that in his fright the horse did not kick the dragging boy.

Espy pulled in beside him, reached down, and with a quick, firm grip yanked Kenny's boot free of the stirrup. The boy slumped to the ground and lay still.

Espy dropped beside him, weakness washing through him, his throat blocked. Gently he lifted the boy's head and brushed the dirt from the still face. His hand was warm and sticky, and not from his own blood.

Sam Kirk had stepped down beside him, while a wide-eyed Joe Kirk sat his horse and held the other three mounts. The loose horses had scattered out into the brush, and the tremor of their hoofbeats still echoed down the draw.

"He's alive." It was Sam Kirk who spoke.

With gentle hands Espy felt over the boy's body. If there were any broken bones, he couldn't find them. But the boy's head was bruised and bleeding.

Sam Kirk stood up, taking the reins of the three held horses. "Joe, you hightail it on to camp. You and the boys throw a mattress and some blankets into the wagon there and get back here just as fast as you can."

"Yes, sir!" Joe wheeled his horse around and spurred across the draw.

Sam tied the horses to nearby bushes, then returned and knelt beside Espy. "Maybe he's just knocked out," he offered in sympathy.

Espy was a long time in finding his voice. "Maybe."

And then there was nothing to do but wait. Wait and think. "I'm obliged to you, Sam. Much obliged."

Yes, he *was* obliged. Whatever he'd intended to do about Sam Kirk would have to wait now. And somehow, Espy was glad.

Espy lifted his head from his hands as Helen Kirk stepped out onto the porch. "He's coming to, Espy."

Espy stood up quickly and pushed through the door after her. He leaned over the bed and took hold of the boy's hand. He forced a smile as Kenny fought to open his eyes.

"How's it going, son?" he spoke, his voice strained.

Kenny's first effort at talking was painful and without success. Finally he managed, "I didn't get thrown off, Dad." Pride was in his voice. "He couldn't have thrown me off . . . if it hadn't been for that big old branch."

Espy squeezed the boy's hand, his eyes burning. "No, son, it was a good ride. He'd've never thrown you off by himself."

Helen Kirk's hand was on Espy's arm, the fingers holding tight. Espy was acutely conscious of them, and he liked them there.

"I think he's going to be all right, Espy," she reassured him. "He's going to hurt for several days, but I think that's all it'll be."

He looked at her warmly. "Thank you, Helen. You've been wonderful."

She smiled, not answering. She walked to the kitchen cabinet and got a bottle. "Sam keeps this around the house for colds and such," she said. "I brought it over. A good stiff drink now might do you a heap of good."

She poured an inch of it into a glass and handed it to him. Hands trembling, Espy took it. It had been a long time, and maybe it would settle his jumbled, tortured nerves.

But something stopped him as the glass touched his lips. The strong, bracing smell of the whisky jerked his head back. He hesitated a moment, then set the glass down.

"No," he said, "for somebody else, maybe. But not for me."

Answering the question in her eyes, he told her, "I fought a long, hard fight with that stuff, Helen, and I won it. But I've got a feeling about it. If I ever took a drink of it, I know I couldn't hold myself back. I'd face that battle all over again."

She nodded sympathetically, putting the bottle back out of sight. "I'm sorry, Espy. I didn't know."

The worry slid away, and weakness rushed in to fill its place. Espy slumped into his chair.

"I'll stay here with him awhile, if you'd like me to, Espy," Helen offered.

Espy nodded. "Thank you, Helen. I'd like you to."

He watched her, and old memories reached up to him, warm, beloved memories.

Mary Bowman had kept to herself since Espy Norwood had arrived, and most especially since the fight. Now, looking out her window, she sensed something amiss at the syndicate house, and sent plump old Delfina to find out.

Still watching out the window, she felt the strong tug of worry, and she wondered about it. Why should she feel any worry about Espy Norwood?

She had every reason to hate him. And indeed she had hated him, or thought so, at least. But somewhere things had changed. Somewhere she had begun to admit to herself that everything he had done so far was in the best interest of the ranch. Not a move could she see that was selfish, or done purely out of malice.

She thought she knew when the change had begun in

her. It was the day she had encouraged Claude Hatch to fight Norwood. From her front porch she had watched, had seen the deep regret which had weighted Norwood's tired face. He had hated the fight, and yet he had gone into it because he had had to, because he was not a coward.

Watching him, she had realized that. And suddenly shame had reached her, a deep, sobering, burning shame. Never had she done such a thing before.

Since that day, she had spent hours at her window, looking for Norwood, and having found him, following him with her penitent eyes. She had wanted him to understand, but never had she been able to make herself go to him and explain. Somehow, perhaps, he would sense what she wanted to say, and would find it in him to forgive her.

When Delfina returned with her report about Kenny, Mary Bowman knew it was time to talk to Norwood, time to empty her heart to him and ease her tortured conscience.

A wave of sympathy swept over her as she walked through the syndicate house door and saw Espy Norwood, his face mirroring the anxious, heartbreaking hours through which he had gone.

Her heart quickening, she said, "I just heard about your boy."

Norwood's eyes lifted to her. She thought she saw softness in them. She hoped she did. "I hope he's not too badly hurt," she said.

He shook his head. "He's going to be all right."

Some of the tension left her in a long breath. "I'm glad of that." Her voice was quiet but earnest. "I'm sorry about a lot of things, Espy. I'm sorry for the way I acted when you first came here."

Norwood's eyes smiled at her. She felt a quick thrill of pleasure.

"I've stayed burrowed up like a badger or something," she went on. "But now I'd like to work with you, help wherever I can."

Visibly surprised, he was pleased nevertheless. She could see that in his gray eyes. It gave her hope. "And, Espy, please forgive me for Claude Hatch."

His head jerked upward. He flinched as if she had hit him. "What do you mean?"

She said, "It was my fault that he fought you. I egged him on. I just didn't realize what I was doing. But I know now, and I'm sorry."

He arose stiffly. No smile was left in his eyes. Of a sudden they had gone hard and cold. "You're sorry." He said it almost like a curse word. "That's easy to say now, that you've almost killed my son."

She took a step backward, her hand raised to her mouth in surprise.

Espy said, "Who do you think it was that we jumped today, running off Figure 4 cattle? I saw them, and so did Sam Kirk.

"One of them was a Wolford man. He was there the day Wolford intercepted me on my way out here. And the other one, Miss Bowman, was Claude Hatch!"

A quick sob clutched her throat. "Espy, I didn't have any idea——"

His fists clenched tightly. His voice cut at her like the sharp edge of a knife. "I forgave you for what you did to me. But how can I forgive you for what you did to my son?"

Tears rushed hot into Mary Bowman's eyes. She whirled and hurried out the door. She shoved into her house, into her room. She fell down across the bed and let the anguished tears come.

She knew now what the matter was. Without wanting to, without even realizing what was happening to her, she had fallen in love with Espy Norwood.

XIV

THE WORD quietly passed through the bunkhouse an hour before daybreak. Only a little muttered conversation rose above the sound of the cowboys pulling on their spurred boots, and the metallic clicking of buckles. Someone threw the bolt on a rifle, and a quiet voice said, "Don't load that thing in here. You're liable to shoot somebody."

Breakfast in the cookshack was unusually quiet. No joking, no hoorawing. Jess Cooley never had a sarcastic word to say.

The men looked up expectantly as Espy Norwood ducked through the low dugout door. Quietly he took his place at the table, the reddish lamplight harshly flickering against his drawn face. A grim determination seemed to be driving him.

Sam Kirk's eyes lifted to the manager's. His shoulders shrugged slightly, and he busied himself with breakfast.

The sound of horses shoving noisily into the corral brought several cowboys to their feet. Finished eating, they moved on out. In a moment the two horse jinglers came in for breakfast.

Most mornings there would be some raucous comment about their horse-handling ability, and a quick answer about some puncher's favorite horse that was going to get forefooted and thrown flat on his back if he didn't quit trying to run off with the whole *remuda*. This morning nobody said anything.

Roping out the morning's mount was accomplished quickly, methodically, and quietly. For several moments Espy had sensed Sam Kirk's eyes upon him. Cinching up, he said over his shoulder, "You don't like this, do you, Sam?"

"Am I supposed to?"

"You don't have to go if you don't want to."

Kirk's answer was blunt. "I'll go wherever my men do."

A slight figure stood at the gate, dimly outlined against the dark sky. Espy led his horse outside, and the figure moved close to him.

Mary Bowman said, "Are you sure you know what you're doing, Espy? Are you sure you're not letting anger over your son drive you into making a mistake?"

He gazed sternly at her. "Who told you what we're going to do?"

"Never mind who. I just want to know if you really think you're right. Has my uncle been stealing Figure 4 cattle?"

Espy said, "I think he has. That's why we're going over there."

"What do you expect to find?"

"Cattle with the Figure 4 on them. Or burnt cattle with the Figure 4 blotted over by some other brand."

Her lips tightened. "And if you find them, what will you do?"

"We'll bring them back. And we'll bring Gid Bowman, too. He'll pay, Mary. Even if he *is* your uncle."

Her gaze was level and unwavering. "He's a leech, Espy. Ever since I was a child, I've hated him. Dad stood for it because they were brothers. The tie was too strong for him to break, I guess. But *I've* broken it."

Her hand hesitantly reached forward, touching his arm. "I'm not worried about Gid Bowman, Espy. I'm worried about *you*."

Espy found himself warming to the touch of her hand, and he didn't want to. Uneasily he pulled his arm back.

She said, "Gid may have Quirt Wolford backing him up."

Espy thought of the beating he had taken, and of the helpless boy who lay in pain at the syndicate house because of Quirt Wolford.

"I hope he does," he said.

Espy swung into the saddle. He tried not to, but he couldn't keep from looking back at her as he swung into a stiff jog trot. The men strung out behind him, two and three abreast. Mary Bowman was left standing alone by the gate, the dust drifting about her. She faded into the predawn darkness.

Espy set an easy pace, one at which the horses could last all day. This was one day they surely would have to.

Try as he might to dismiss her from his mind, his thoughts dwelt stubbornly upon Mary Bowman. Again and again he heard her phantom voice. There had been a worrisome sincerity in the way she spoke, worrisome because it didn't fit with her sending Wolford to beat him.

More than once she had denied having done that. Now Espy was finding it harder and harder to convince himself that she had.

In some obscure way, it had pleased him that she had walked out to talk to him this morning. He could almost imagine he still felt the touch of her hand upon his arm. He forgot for a while about her being Mary Bowman, an enemy to him. He found himself thinking of her only as a woman, a very desirable woman. And the thought eased the hardset lines in his face, bringing warmth to his chill gray eyes.

The morning was far gone when Espy reined in and waited for the stragglers to catch up. To Sam Kirk he said, "This is about where Gid's country starts, isn't it?"

When Sam nodded, Espy went on, "All right, we'll drop the first man off right here. Next man a quarter mile farther, and so on till we're strung out all the way across. Then we'll ride due south, taking it slow and easy and combing the brush for cattle. If you find anything that looks halfway kin to a Figure 4, push it along.

"We'll work south ten miles, then all shove whatever we find toward the center, at the south end of Gid's range. If anybody stumbles into trouble, fire into the air. The rest of us will come running. Any questions?"

There were none. Espy nodded to the old puncher named Dolph. "Dolph, if you'll drop off here——" It was always wise to have a steady hand on the outside of a drive.

Espy struck due west then, dropping the men off one by one. In time he reached the western end of Gid Bowman's range, and only Sam Kirk was left with him. For quite a while Sam had eyed him expectantly every time he had stopped. But never had Espy chosen to drop the foreman off.

For Espy, the reason was simple enough. He didn't trust Sam. And from the frosty reserve in the foreman's face, he knew Kirk sensed it.

Espy edged his horse southward. "Let's go, Sam. We've got the longest ride to make."

He hadn't expected to find anything at first, so it didn't worry him. But when he had ridden an hour, then two, without finding anything but a few scattered cattle carrying Bowman's brand, it began to nettle him. From an occasional high point he would watch for the other riders, and having found them, try to see whether or not they were pushing any cattle along. So far as he could tell, they weren't.

He took off his hat and wiped his forehead with his sleeve, wondering whether it was the heat or the growing tug of worry that brought the sweat.

The sun was beginning to edge downward from its peak when Espy saw the single rider angling across toward him, his horse in a lope. For one moment Espy's pulse quickened. *They've found something,* he thought.

Then the rider drew closer, and recognition came. Espy's mouth pulled downward at the corners. He stopped, his hand fisted on the reins.

Gid Bowman hauled up so close that he could almost reach out and strike Espy. "What the hell do you think you're doing, Norwood? Get your men off of my range!" Though red-eyed and flushed, he was stone sober this time. And he was madder than a cat in a washtub.

Espy said flatly, "We're looking for Figure 4 cattle."

"If any of your cattle stray onto my land, I'll send them back to you. You don't catch me on *your* range."

Espy almost smiled at that. "No, but we've tried to."

Bowman flamed at the insult. "Get your men off, Norwood. Get them off before I go fetch the law."

Espy said, "What law—Llewellyn? We'll be through and gone before you can sober him up."

Bowman's hand trembled on his bridle reins. "Norwood, I warn you——" His eyes cut sharply to Sam Kirk. "Make him leave, Sam. If you don't, you'll wish *you'd* left a long time ago."

Kirk stiffened.

Espy sensed the angry understanding that passed

between the two men. "What do you mean by that, Bowman?"

Bowman said, "Sam knows."

Kirk's eyes blazed, but they avoided Espy. Espy vainly studied the foreman's rigid face. He found no answer there, but he thought he knew the answer, just the same.

His voice cut like a razor, "We're going to ride your ranch out, Bowman. I know you've been stealing Figure 4 cattle. Frank Bowman must've known it, too, but he wouldn't take action because you were his brother. So you got away with it. But not anymore. If we find any stolen cattle here, we'll be back, looking for *you*. Come on, Sam."

He pulled his horse away and headed south again, leaving the bristling Gid Bowman to mutter to himself.

Espy and Kirk rode another hour, and still they found nothing. Espy paused often to listen for the bawl of cattle to the east of him, sound which would indicate that other riders were pushing along Figure 4 cattle. He heard nothing except the breathing of his horse and the quiet creak of his saddle.

He started the circle, swinging eastward again, sweeping the lower end of Bowman's range. But even as he did, he knew instinctively that the drive had been for nothing. He squinted hard, hoping he would see cattle gathering far up yonder. But somehow, he knew he wouldn't.

One by one the cowboys began falling in closer to him as they worked toward the center. Past midafternoon, they all met. Espy's eyes swept them. He didn't have to ask. He could tell.

His jaw clenched, and he slapped his saddle horn with the flat of his hand, jarring loose at least a little of the galling anger. He could taste the frustration, sour as vinegar.

"There *had* to be something," he gritted in protest. "Didn't anybody find *anything?*"

Some of the men shook their heads, the rest didn't have to. Espy glanced at Sam Kirk and thought he saw relief ease into the foreman's face.

The breath went out of Espy in a long, almost inaudible sigh. He shrugged helplessly. "They've moved south, then. And I reckon we're whipped for now. Let's get started home."

Instead of taking the lead this time, he dropped back to the rear, his shoulders slumped.

Damn it, he knew he'd been right. Gid Bowman was guilty, that was as certain as the prairie wind. And they hadn't found a thing. But one of them *had* found something.

Cotton Dulaney hipped around in the saddle and looked back at Espy. The kid could see the bitter twist of frustration in the manager's face.

Maybe I ought to tell him, he thought.

But he wouldn't. He'd made up his mind to that. This was *his* discovery, Cotton's alone.

He'd get a chance in a day or two. Then he'd ease back down here and follow up what he had found. A big bunch of riders could never hope to slip up on those cow thieves. But one man, alone, might.

The thought of it brought a happy surge of warmth. *I won't ever be the kid of this outfit again.*

For two days Matt Ollinger had roamed what passed for streets in Mobeetie. He had been in every bar, and there were several of them. He had listened to all the gossip he could pick up concerning Espy Norwood and the Figure 4. And all the time he expectantly watched the trail which led in from the north, and wondered why in sin a woman had to be so damn slow.

The more he heard about the Figure 4, the more

worried he got. A big outfit, and a long way from town.
It wouldn't be easy to slip in there, steal a kid, and get
clean away. Especially when you didn't know the country. It began to look like he was going to have to enlist
some help.

Then Lady Luck dealt him a royal flush. Standing by
the grimy front window of one of the saloons, he saw a
rider knee a big brown horse toward a hitch rack.
Ollinger's whiskers lifted in a slow grin as his boot heel
ground his cigarette on the dirt floor, and he walked out
into the morning sun.

"Jake!" he said, his voice hardly lifting above a
normal tone. "Jake Claymore!"

The rider hauled up short, quickly on the defensive.
Recognition came and he relaxed, reining in beside
Ollinger. He reached down to take the man's hand.

"Name's Smith now," Claymore said pleasantly.
"Just plain old Smith. How you doing, Matt?"

"Still using my own name."

Early though it was, they had a drink together, and
then two. Ollinger pumped Claymore for information,
and he finally got it out of him that he was working with
Quirt Wolford.

"Wolford," Ollinger mused, fingering his dark
whiskers. "I've been hearing about him. Might be he's
just the man to help me with a deal I got rigged up."

Claymore shrugged. "I don't know. Quirt's got his
hands pretty full right now. But if there was money in
it . . ."

"There's not any money in the deal," Ollinger lied.
"But I thought maybe Wolford might like to help me
with it anyhow. It'd give him a chance to even up with
Norwood. Sometimes there's things you can't just put a
price tag on. Some things are worth doing when there
ain't a nickel in them."

Claymore skeptically shook his head. "I don't

know. You can't ever tell about Quirt Wolford. He's a smart man, Matt, a mighty smart man. Yet once in a while he acts like he's crazy.''

Ollinger signaled for another drink. ''Take me to him, Jake. Let me talk with him.''

Worriedly Claymore said, ''I don't dare do that, Matt. Quirt would shoot us both if I took a stranger to his camp.''

''I'm not a stranger, Jake, not to you. You can vouch for me. If he likes the idea, fine. If he doesn't, I'll leave. You know how I stand with the law. You know I wouldn't tell anybody a thing I seen.''

Claymore frowned deeply. With misgivings he finally gave in. ''All right, Matt. But just remember it was your own idea.''

Ollinger grinned. ''Stop worrying. There ain't nothing going to happen.''

Cotton Dulaney paused in the edge of the brush, trying to get his bearings. He looked wistfully at the hill yonder. If he could get on top of that, he could find his way for sure. But he'd be seen for sure, too. He had to keep to the brush.

He could find the place all right, if he could just spot that old dead cottonwood he'd seen beside a creek bed. The giant tree had been split down the middle by a bolt of lightning sometime in the past. Now its gaunt, stricken branches stood starkly against the skyline like a lonely grave marker far out on the prairie.

Cotton kept riding, sticking close to the protecting brush and watching carefully for the tree. He smiled as he thought how pleased Espy Norwood and Sam Kirk were going to be. Oh, they might paw a little sand because he went out alone. But at least they would have to accept him as a man now.

He found the fire-struck tree. Excitement began to

play through him like electricity through a cat's fur in
storm time. Straight east, a quarter of a mile.

He made the quarter mile with his hand on his .44.
He had long since checked his saddle gun. It too was
loaded and ready.

He found the place. It was just as he had left it the
other day. Here was a small clearing in the midst of the
brush. Inside it was a single pole corral, built of cedar
and mesquite and anything else that had come to hand.

Quickly Cotton's eyes searched for sign that anyone
had been here since he had discovered the place. Evidently no one had.

Disappointment was keen and painful. He *had* to
find something.

Cotton kicked at the old trace of branding fires. A
thin layer of dust had settled over the black ashes. The
place hadn't been used in several days, maybe several
weeks. It might even have been left for good.

He found the smoke-blackened running iron lying
just where he had seen it before. He picked it up and
knocked the loose dirt off against the fence. This was a
typical rustler's iron, all right. Short enough that a man
could carry it on his saddle without trouble, without its
even being particularly noticeable. And the curved,
J-shaped end of it was made for running a new brand
over an old one.

For a moment Cotton considered taking the running
iron back for his proof. But he could have done *that*
well the other day. No, it wasn't enough. All he would
get would be a thorough chewing-out for coming back
here by himself. He had to do better.

He tied the running iron to his saddle and headed
south. By George, he *would* find something, or he
wouldn't go back. He'd ride all the way down to the
Colorado River, if he had to.

He didn't have to. At dusk he hobbled his horse, ate a

little from the sack of food he had stolen out of Jess Cooley's kitchen, and lay down on the ground, his head against his saddle. At sunup he was in the saddle again. Before long he began to run across cattle sign—fresh sign.

The sound of bawling cattle reached him. He'd cowboyed long enough to know that cattle being driven don't sound like cattle free on the range. And these were being driven.

Staying in the brush, he got close enough to see the herd. It was a little bunch, mostly young heifers, some cows with their first calves. He couldn't see the brand, but he knew the underbit earmark. Figure 4!

Cotton's heartbeat quickened. For the first time he knew the sudden grip of real fear, and a true realization of his position here began to sink in. Gone was the kid excitement, the lighthearted search for glory. Soberly he admitted to himself that he stood a good chance of getting killed.

Now was the time to turn back, to go for help.

But he couldn't do it, not yet. He had to see where these cattle were being taken. What good was it to know where they came from, but not where they went?

He licked dry lips and edged his horse forward. He'd dealt into the game. Now he would play out his hand.

Matt Ollinger rubbed a sleeve across his sweaty face. "You said it was a far piece, Jake," he grumbled, "but you didn't say it was halfway to Mexico."

Jake Claymore—or Smith—shifted his weight in the saddle. "It's not far now. Just around the hill a little ways."

Ollinger grunted. He was beginning to think it had been a mistake to come all the way out here. What if he couldn't get Wolford interested? One thing sure, he wasn't going to split any money with him. Five hundred dollars wasn't much when you had to share it.

Claymore said, "Wonder whose horse that is yonder?"

Ollinger's eyes followed his. He had almost missed the animal, tied out in the brush. Riding in close, he saw that it was a young pony, probably not much more than a bronc. And burned on its hip was a Figure 4.

Claymore jumped to the ground, gun in his hand, and began to move swiftly afoot, following the boot tracks that led away from the horse. Ollinger tied his own horse and followed.

The bawling of the cattle grew louder as they cautiously traced the tracks. They both saw the cowboy at the same time. Bellied down under a thick, low-growing mesquite, he was watching the men in a corral a hundred or so yards away, changing Figure 4 brands into something that looked like an Arrowhead.

Ollinger said sharply, "Get up slow and turn this way."

The cowboy jerked in surprise. He saw two guns leveled in his face. The color drained from his cheeks. Why, this was nothing more than a kid, Ollinger saw.

"Get up," he said.

The young cowboy slowly complied, his hands unsteady. His eyes were wild, and Ollinger read the thought behind them.

"Don't try it, kid. We'd kill you before you took two steps."

Cotton Dulaney gave up then. Ollinger saw the .44 at the boy's hip and the saddle gun he had leaned against a low limb of the tree. The youngster's hardware had been ready, but the boy hadn't.

With an old back-trail instinct, Ollinger knew Quirt Wolford without having to be told. Jake Claymore quickly explained to Wolford how they had come upon Cotton's horse.

Glaring malevolently, Wolford struck the boy across the face with the back of his hand. The impact knocked the kid's hat off, exposing a tangle of cottony hair. "How many others out there?" he demanded.

Cotton involuntarily raised his hand to his mouth, in an effort to hold the pain. "They're all there," he said desperately. "Enough of them to wipe you out. You better let me go."

Wolford studied him. "You're lying." He slapped the boy again. "You came by yourself."

That blow drew blood. Cotton stood silent, his hand over his mouth. Wolford ordered a couple of his men to go after Cotton's horse, as well as Claymore's and Ollinger's. In a few minutes they were back.

"Any sign of others?" Wolford asked. They shook their heads.

Wolford turned back to the boy. "Just got a little too big for your britches, didn't you, kid? You should've stayed home, where you belonged. Now you're never going back."

He reached for Cotton's rope and shook it down.

One of Wolford's men stepped forward. "Wait a minute, Wolford. What're you fixing to do?"

Wolford turned on him angrily. "Go back to the branding pen, Hatch."

Fear looked out of Claude Hatch's eyes. "He's just a kid, Quirt. Let him go."

"Let him go and get us hung?" Wolford stepped into Cotton's saddle. He dropped a loop over the boy's shoulders and spurred the horse. Cotton cried out once, and only once.

Moments later Wolford came back, dragging the limp body. The excited bronc stepped along fearfully, its eyes rolling. A couple of the men turned their backs and walked away. Even Matt Ollinger felt a flutter at the pit of his stomach. He carefully avoided looking down the rope.

Quirt Wolford was the only man who seemed unaffected. His voice was even as he dismounted. "Jake, we got to take this kid back to Figure 4 range and dump him. Turn the horse loose and leave the rope dragging. It'll look like an accident."

Claymore's face was the color of clabber. "Like that Englishman Spence?"

"Yes. Just like him."

The sound of a horse's hoofs jerked Wolford around. Claude Hatch had mounted and was riding away. "Come back here," Wolford bawled at him.

The cowboy rode on, unmindful. Wolford drew his gun and fired just over Hatch's head. Hatch hauled up. He pulled the horse around and came back at a slow walk. His whole frame was atremble with horror at what he had seen.

Wolford pointed to the torn body of Cotton Dulaney. "Take a look, Hatch, a good look. If you ever try to run out on me, that's what'll happen to *you!*"

Hatch dragged back to the branding pen and leaned over the fence, sick.

Wolford's angry eyes flicked over the rest of the men. "All right, now, get on back to the pen and finish up. We got a lot to do."

When the rest had gone to work, Wolford walked up to Ollinger. "Matt Ollinger," he said evenly. "I've heard of you. Now, what kind of a deal have you got?"

XV

COTTON DULANEY was carried to the Figure 4's little burial ground atop a hill overlooking the headquarters. The circuit-riding minister finished his short funeral sermon, and the solemn cowboys filed by one by one to empty a shovel of dirt into the grave. With them was Arch McCavitt, his red hair bared to the gentle wind.

Jess Cooley stood off to one side, his back turned. Espy placed his hand on the cook's shoulder and felt the thin old frame shake.

The Kirk family stood together. Kenny Norwood was with them, beside Joe Kirk. Except for a little lingering soreness, Kenny had recovered.

Mary Bowman stood alone, by the wooden cross which had been erected over her father's grave not many weeks before. Her small hands crumpled a handkerchief. Several times Espy had sensed her eyes touching him. Now he felt compelled to stand beside her.

"The service is over, Mary," he said presently. "I'd like to walk back down with you."

Her eyes lifted to him. They brimmed with tears, unreserved and unashamed.

"Thank you, Espy. I'd like you to."

For half the distance down the hill they walked without speaking. Espy felt her nearness bringing an awakening warmth.

"He was a good kid," Espy said.

Mary nodded. "Dad was always fond of him. Next

to Sam Kirk and Jess Cooley, I guess Cotton was his favorite.''

Memory brought a near smile, momentarily relaxing her pretty face. ''I'll never forget when Cotton came here, about three years ago. Just a half-starved, freckle-faced kid who didn't have a home anywhere until Dad gave him one. He had turned up in Mobeetie with a freight outfit, ragged and hungry, and somehow he had wound up at Arch McCavitt's. They always do. Arch fed him a few days, bought him new clothes, and set him up to an old saddle somebody had left there. Then Arch sent Cotton out here.''

Her slight shoulders slacked. Espy put his arm around them. Touching her sent an electric tingle through him. He started to take his arm away but didn't. He wondered vaguely what had happened to the bitterness he had borne toward her. It was gone. Now all he had was an aching desire to hold her tighter. With some effort, he restrained that.

At the door she turned to face him, and regretfully he drew his arm away. But her warm fingers closed upon his hand. Her eyes leveled softly with his. ''Espy,'' she said, ''I wish . . .''

''Wish what?''

She hesitated. ''Nothing, I guess. Please come in, Espy. I'll fix some coffee.''

He followed her into the big rock house and back into the kitchen. He leaned against the cabinet, letting his eyes trail her as she ground coffee beans, dipped water into the small coffeepot, and put it on the stove. Watching her, he felt an old loneliness sweep over him again. Helen Kirk had awakened it in him, bringing up old and comfortable memories that had long remained unstirred. He hadn't been in love with Helen Kirk, he knew that. It was simply that with her he had realized more keenly than ever before how gray and empty life had become for him the last few years, how empty it was likely to be as time went on. Sure, he had a son, and that was a great help. But a man needed more—much more.

He didn't intend to do it. But without realizing what he was doing until he had done it, he caught the girl's shoulders and pulled her into his arms.

For a second her lips were tight with surprise. Then they softened. She answered his kiss with warmth, her loving hands tight on his back, her breasts soft against him.

When their lips parted, she pressed her cheek to his chest, her hands still holding him. Espy's arms remained tight around her.

"I didn't intend to do that, Mary," he said. "I don't know what came over me."

Softly she said, "I think I know, Espy. And I'm glad."

After a while Arch McCavitt came looking for him. Standing in the front door, he stared first at Mary, then at Espy, as if he didn't know whether to grin or frown.

"Jess Cooley's got something to tell you, Espy," he said in a solemn voice. "You better go with me."

Jess Cooley didn't see them as they first walked into the saddle shed. The old cook was talking quietly to the two boys, Joe and Kenny. Cooley fondly placed his hand on Joe Kirk's head, tousling the sandy-colored hair.

"Joe," he said, "that old saddle of yours is a worn-out wreck. Cotton thought a heap of you, and he'd have wanted you to have his. Take it, son."

Joe's eyes were shining. Reverently he reached out and touched Cotton's saddle. It was almost a new one. Choking, he said, "Gosh, Jess. Thanks."

The old cook's voice wavered. "Don't thank me. Just always remember Cotton, and try to be as good a hand as he was. That'll be thanks enough."

He became aware of Espy and Arch. His face went grim. "Let's go outside, Espy. I've found something."

The old man's hand clasped a short piece of iron. Outside, away from the boys, Jess Cooley suddenly turned and said. "It wasn't no accident, Espy. Cotton was murdered!"

Espy stopped abruptly, missing a breath. Chilling, he stared at Cooley. "How do you know, Jess?"

Cooley's narrowed eyes were crackling. "After the funeral, Dolph and me stayed on the hill to put up a cross. Dolph got to telling me how he found Cotton. I hadn't heard it before, because I hadn't been able to listen. This time I *did* listen.

"Dolph found the kid down toward the south end, on that big, open flat. There wasn't no brush there, Espy. None for a long ways. But it was me that dressed the kid for burial, and I could tell he'd been drug through the brush. There was thorns and twigs and . . ."

The old man's throat bobbed. His tough old fists drew up like mesquite knots. "He didn't die where Dolph found him. He was drug to death someplace else, and his body was moved."

Espy stared at the ground, fury scorching his face like a white-hot iron.

Cooley steadied his voice. "Something else, Espy. I found this tied to his saddle." He held forth the short object he had kept in his hand.

"A running iron," Espy said.

Cooley nodded. "I didn't think much of it at first. It ain't uncommon for folks to carry them. I figured he just happened to find it someplace. But now—I reckon we all know where he found it."

Espy's flaming eyes met Cooley's, then flicked to

Arch. His hand went back to his hip, where the pistol usually rode. "We'll find him, Jess," he spoke grimly. "I'll get the boys together, and we won't come back till Quirt Wolford is dead!"

He whirled and started for the bunkhouse. Arch grabbed his arm, jerking him to a halt. "Wait a minute, Espy. That's not the way. I've already talked it over with Jess and made him see. Now *you've* got to see. This is for the law to handle."

Angrily Espy snapped, "The law? Like that sot Llewellyn?"

Earnestly Arch said, "Yes, the law, but not like Llewellyn. We've had an election in town since you were there. The old sheriff resigned. The new one's been hoping for a chance to get something on Wolford. This is his chance. Leave it to him, Espy. Wolford will hang, all right. Let him hang legal.

"That'll show we've finally got a law that means something. It'll do more to run the thieves out than a dozen lynching bees could."

Although his face was dark, Espy studied that. "Arch, I wouldn't've thought *you'd* ever be the one to give me a speech like that."

Arch said, "I'd never've thought I'd ever have to."

Espy could see that Arch was dead serious about this. He looked at Jess. The cook seemed to have been convinced. After a minute Espy gave in. "All right, Arch. I'll send somebody after the sheriff."

Arch shook his head. "You won't have to. I've already sent the minister."

Wryly Espy said, "You're ahead of me every jump."

"I figured if was better if we didn't let the cowboys know till the sheriff was here. You know what they'd want to do. Just exactly what you'd started to, Espy."

Espy rubbed the back of his neck. "I reckon you're right, Arch. We'll give the law a try. But just one. If it doesn't pan out in a hurry, we'll handle this ourselves."

Arch nodded. "Fair enough, I guess. The new sheriff is a friend of mine, Espy. This'll give him a chance to prove himself."

After a bit, Jess Cooley hobbled off toward the cookshack. Espy looked toward Sam Kirk's house up the slope. He straightened in resignation, knowing what he had to do.

"I'll see you after a while, Arch. Right now I've got a job."

Helen Kirk answered his knock. "I'm looking for Sam," he told her.

She managed a smile, though her face was drawn. "He's here, Espy."

Sam stepped out upon the porch, and Espy motioned for him to follow. They walked together to the syndicate house. Sam's face was haggard. It was evident that Cotton's death had hit him hard.

Espy made it quick and blunt. "Cotton didn't die by accident, Sam. Quirt Wolford murdered him. We've got the proof."

Sam's chin hardened, but he didn't look too surprised. "I guess I knew it. I tried to believe it wasn't so."

Espy tightened his fist. "I want you to leave, Sam, Now. Today!"

Sam's leathery cheeks lost their color.

Espy said, "I know you're tied in with Wolford some way, Sam. There's no need for you to deny it. But I know you wouldn't have had a hand in getting Cotton killed. And I owe you something, for Kenny. So I'm giving you a chance to get away, before the sheriff gets here."

Whatever was going on in Sam's mind, his guarded eyes never betrayed it.

"I hate to leave, Espy."

"But you will, Sam. If you don't, I won't protect you."

"I'd have to tell Helen something . . . and Joe."

"That's up to you. But tell them something and get out of here, Now!"

For a long time Sam stared out the open door, his hands flat against the seams of his saddle-worn trousers. Evidently reaching a decision, he faced Espy again. "You're a good man, Espy. I'd like to've been friends with you, if things had been different. Now it's too late, I reckon."

He extended his hand. *"Adios,* Espy."

Espy's throat tightened as he watched Sam go. Yes, Sam was right. If things *had* been different . . .

Espy walked out of the house and down toward the saddle shed again. Arch fell in beside him. Each sensed the melancholy that gripped the other. There was no need for talk between them. It was enough just to walk side by side, tied by a bond from long ago.

Aimlessly they moved past the saddle shed and up the slope to the bubbling spring that had drawn Frank Bowman to this place years ago, when this was still grazing ground for the buffalo, and when the Comanche still hunted here for meat, and for horses, and even for scalps. For a long while Espy and Arch sat there upon a big stone and stared silently at the rushing water, each with his own thoughts.

Restlessly Arch pitched pebbles into the water, watching the tiny splash of white after each one. Presently he said. "Mary Bowman's in love with you, isn't she, Espy?"

Half-startled, Espy said, "Why?"

"I saw her watching you at the funeral today. I could

tell. And while ago at her house, when I went to get you . . .''

He paused. "I think a lot of that girl, Espy. I hope you're not going to hurt her. Are you in love with her?''

Espy colored. "Arch, I don't know. I think I am. But I can't be sure. How can I know if it's really her, or if it's just that I'm lonely—that it's been so long since I've had any real interest in a woman that I'm letting my imagination run away with me?''

"Hasn't any woman ever stirred you since you lost Jeannie?''

"Sure, I've found myself interested several times, the way any man is apt to be drawn to a pretty woman. But it takes more than that, Arch. For me it does. There's never been one since Jeannie that hit me like this girl has.''

Arch gripped Espy's shoulder. "Well, Espy, I hope this is the one. For you and for her. You both deserve the best. And I think you've both got it.''

Arch stood up and stretched his long frame. Looking down toward the buildings, he suddenly frowned. "Here comes Helen Kirk, And something's got her excited.''

Espy quickly arose and turned around. Helen was half running up the slope toward them, her face stricken. In long strides Espy hurried down to meet her.

Breathing heavily, she cried, "Espy, I've been looking everywhere for you. Sam's gone.''

Regretfully Espy nodded. "I know.'' So Sam hadn't told her.

"But his guns, Espy. Why did he take his guns?''

"Guns?''

Trying desperately to keep from sobbing, she said, "Yes, his guns. He's gone to kill somebody, Espy. I could tell by the way he acted. He said he was going to do a job he should have done a long time ago.''

Espy's blood chilled. His eyes met Arch's, and both men had the same answer.

"I tried to stop him," Helen cried, "but he wouldn't listen. He said someday I'd understand."

Espy gripped her cold hand. "Don't worry, Helen. I'll catch up with him and bring him back."

"He has a long start," she said. "It took me a while to find you."

"I'll bring him back," Espy said again. Then he struck into a long run down the slope and toward the saddle shed. Arch was right behind him.

While Espy roped a loose horse out of a corral, Arch asked him, "How did you know Sam was gone?"

"Because I fired him. I told him to leave. But I didn't count on a thing like this."

Briefly he explained what had happened. Arch listened patiently, then shook his head.

"You shouldn't have done it, Espy. You were wrong, dead wrong."

Incredulously, Espy stared, trying to read what was in Arch's mind.

Arch said, "Sam Kirk is a good man, Espy, a better man than you know."

"But the tallies, Arch."

Arch thought. *I know about the tallies. I know a lot more too. But the people out here have been my friends for years, Espy. It's not my place to tell you what I know. You'll have to find out for yourself.*

He said, "Believe me, Espy you've made a mistake about Sam Kirk."

Looking into his friend's face, Espy realized Arch was telling the truth even though he hadn't given his reasons. He felt a quick wash of relief. He knew that, all along, he had wanted to believe Sam innocent.

Arch's horse was in the corral, too. Quickly Arch caught and saddled him.

Espy demanded, "What do you think *you're* doing?"

"Sam's *my* friend as well as yours. I'm going to help you find him and bring him back."

A thin smile came to Espy's face. "Been a long time since we've ridden together, Arch."

Arch nodded. "And let's get at it."

XVI

THE APPROACH of darkness never slowed Sam Kirk's determined pace. As daylight faded, a blood-red moon slowly arose. The stars blinked into view—one, two, half a dozen, and then the whole sky glittered, Sam knew his direction.

The full moon had risen high and night had polished it to a bright silver when Sam at last struck Gid Bowman's own trail. He reined in upon it and followed its southward course in an easy jog trot. The prairie wind had diminished to a cooling night breeze, carrying with it the warbling call of a night bird and the brittle staccato of a cricket.

As he rode, Sam's mind dwelt upon Cotton Dulaney. His hand went to his gun again and again.

At last Gid Bowman's cluttered camp broke into view before him, the low-built dugouts hardly casting a shadow in the brilliant moonlight. Sam dismounted, leading his horse to keep him from kicking up a racket among the castaway tin cans and rubbish that littered the place. He tied the horse to an abandoned wagon, then went on to Bowman's living quarters afoot. Gun in hand, he cautiously walked down the shaky steps and ducked through the open door. For a moment he stood still, trying to identify the vague black shapes he could see scattered about the stuffy room. From the corner came the rasping sound of one man's snoring. *One man.*

Sam struck a match and lighted a smoky lamp. One glance in the flickering light confirmed that Bowman was alone.

"Wake up, Gid," he spoke curtly.

The snoring broke off abruptly. Gid Bowman sat up sleepy-eyed on his cot.

"Get your pants on, Gid," Sam said. "We're going for a ride."

It took a moment for the idea to force its way into Bowman's muddled brain. "A ride? In the middle of the night? Anyway, what in the hell do you think you're doing here, Sam?"

Kirk's voice was grim. "You're going to take me to Quirt Wolford. We're leaving right now. Get your pants on or you'll go in your underwear."

Grumbling, Gid Bowman swung his legs over the side of the cot. He scratched his sides, put on his hat and his boots, then pulled on his pants. Lastly he put on his shirt, shoving the tail of it into the ample waistband of his low-fitting trousers.

"You're crazy, Sam," he said, his eyes on the gun in the foreman's hand. "Quirt won't ever let you get to his camp."

Sam said, "He'll let me, because you're going to take me."

"And if I don't?"

Sam's eyes were brittle. He poked the gun into Bowman's soft belly. "You will."

Bowman had left a night horse in a corral. Punched up by Sam's gun, he saddled him and the two men rode southward. Sam pitched his rope around Gid's middle and knotted it. The other end he dallied around his own saddle horn.

"Try anything and I'll bounce your fat rump all over this ranch."

Gid Bowman no longer blustered. Fear put a tremor

in his voice. ''What do you say we at least wait for daylight?''

''No. There'll be men following me. And they can't follow in the dark.''

Much later, far up in the dead hours after midnight, they halted to rest the horses. Sam never slept, watching Bowman. And Bowman never slept, watching Sam's gun.

''Sam,'' he asked once, ''just what do you figure to do if we get there?''

Sam's voice was deadly as the rattle of a diamondback. ''I'm going to kill Quirt Wolford!''

As daylight came, Sam pulled back into the brush, following Gid Bowman southward. ''How much farther, Gid?''

''A good ride yet. But you better turn back while you can, Sam. You'll never make it.''

''I'll make it.'' Sam frowned. ''You know what happened to Cotton Dulaney?''

Cautiously Bowman said, ''I've heard tell.''

''He was dragged to death. It was an awful sight.'' Sam jerked at the rope around Gid's belly, jerked hard enough to make the heavy man grunt.

''I'm tying the rope to my saddle horn, Gid. If anything happens to me, my horse will run away. And he'll drag you with him, just the way Cotton was drug. So you better see that nothing happens to me.''

Bowman's heavy face went the color of flour paste. His wide shoulders slumped. The hope went out of him.

They stopped and rested for one long period during the day, under the cover of brush. They had changed directions frequently, Bowman insisting that they were going the right way. When Sam figured the horses had had enough rest, he swung into his saddle. Bowman started to remount.

"No, Gid," Sam said curtly, taking the bridle reins. "You've led me miles out of the way. But you're not going to do it again. You're going to walk and lead me. Every extra mile you go means blisters on your feet."

Rage bubbled into Bowman's helpless face. He hobbled southwestward, Sam trailing behind him, the rope still on his saddle horn. Sam knew that this time they were headed the right way.

It was near night when Gid Bowman nervously reined up. Sam had finally let him mount again and ride.

"We're almost there," Bowman spoke nervously. "About three or four hundred yards ahead yonder, just off of the draw."

Sam swung down. "All right, then, we'll go the rest of the way afoot. You tie your horse here."

Bowman did. "Now, how about this rope?" he asked querulously.

Sam shook his head. "It stays on till I know you're not trying to trick me. I'll lead my horse. And don't you forget for a minute, he's plenty shy."

Staying well within the cover of the brush, they slowly worked forward. Sam stayed ready to cover the horse's nostrils at any sign it might nicker. The clanging of iron reached Sam's ears. He recognized it as a Dutch oven lid being dropped into place.

"You didn't lie this time, Gid. You can untie that rope now."

With nervous fingers Bowman slipped off the rope. Then he looked up at Sam Kirk. His eyes suddenly widened, and his mouth dropped open. His startled cry broke short as Sam swung his gun barrel down and took Bowman behind the ear.

Bowman sprawled out and lay limp on the grass. Kirk looked down at the unconscious man without pity. "Just for safety, Gid," he breathed.

Sam tied his horse and moved toward the sound he had heard. More camp noise reached him as he went ahead—the clatter of tin plates, the lift of conversation, the stamping of hoofs, and the occasional bawling of a cow or calf.

In the edge of the brush he lay flat on his belly to study the camp in the waning daylight. He could count half a dozen men eating supper around a campfire. Cut into a bank nearby was a dugout, and close beside it was an aging corral of rocks and brush. An old abandoned buffalo hunters' camp, most likely.

In vain he sought Quirt Wolford. The only man he knew there was Claude Hatch. Sam's teeth clenched momentarily as he watched the one-time Figure 4 cowboy, sitting apart from the others, picking disconsolately at a meal that seemed to have no taste for him.

I hope it chokes you, Sam thought bitterly.

Then Sam's heartbeat quickened as Quirt Wolford stepped out of the dugout. From the way the men all stopped eating to look at him, Sam sensed that they were afraid of him. Even at that distance, he could feel the dread that followed the outlaw as he walked toward the cookfire.

Another man came out behind Wolford. He was much the same size and of much the same bearing. He spoke carelessly to Wolford, as an equal. Sam sensed that here was the only man in camp who was not in fear of the band's leader. He was a gunman, that was plain from the way he wore a double set of .45s, low and tied to his legs.

Carefully Sam raised his gun and rested it in the low fork of a mesquite tree. His heart hammering dully, he licked his lips and drew a careful bead on Wolford as the big man leaned over a Dutch oven, then straightened with two biscuits in his hand. For two long seconds Sam squeezed on the trigger.

Then, scowling, his finger released the pressure. Too far. He wished he had brought a rifle.

He had to get closer. For a time he scanned the camp, looking for a way to get closer without being seen. He thought he saw it. By backing into the brush and skirting around a deep, flood-cut arroyo, he could get behind the dugout and creep in by the old rock corral.

Five minutes later he was crouched behind the piled-up rocks, carefully searching for Wolford.

Excitement burned within him like tall grass afire. He had to be quick. Gid Bowman was likely to come out of it any minute, and he would come out yelling.

But Sam held back, trying to make his plan. He had only a half-formed one in his mind. Main thing was to kill Wolford. After that, he'd take care of himself the best way he could. Maybe the men wouldn't put up much of a fight. He was hoping for that. But if they did, and luck stayed with him, maybe he could hold them off until darkness gave him a chance to get away.

Wolford sat cross-legged on the ground, eating out of a tin plate. At this angle, sitting sideways to Sam, he made a poor target. A bullet fired from here would strike him in the arm. It wasn't likely to be fatal. Sam had to inch around for a better position. Anxiety began to beat at him like a club beating a rug on a line.

At last Wolford stood up. Sam's breath caught. He leveled the gun across the top of the rock fence, waiting for Wolford to turn.

Then it happened. From across the campfire, in the brush, an excited voice called, "Quirt, look out! Kirk's there somewhere, and he's trying to kill you!"

It was Gid Bowman's voice. In desperation Sam squeezed the trigger and missed. Wolford broke into a run, whipping out his gun and firing back as he sped for cover.

Some of the rustlers were caught without their guns.

But enough of them were armed that the fence instantly became a beehive of snarling bullets, smashing into the rocks or striking them at an angle and whining away into the dusk.

In bitter disappointment Sam crouched low and tried to reach better cover. But bullets kicked up dust around him and drove him back. He was hemmed in. All he had was the fence, and a steep bank behind it.

His heart sank in despair. He had had his chance, and it had slipped through his fingers like water. Maybe he could get out of here, maybe he couldn't. Whether he did nor not, Quirt Wolford was still alive. Sam knew he wouldn't get another chance at him.

He crawled back into a corner where they would have less chance of getting at him from behind. And there he waited, firing only when he saw something to fire at, trying to watch in front of him and behind him at the same time. He watched the dusky blue of the skies deepen into the black of night. It seemed that it was taking forever.

Then they rushed him. Above the hammering of gunfire he heard Quirt Wolford urging the men on, heard him hollering something about getting Sam before dark.

Sweat cold and clammy on his face and on his hands, Sam used both guns, the one he always carried in his holster and a second one he had jammed into his waistband before he rode away from the Figure 4. He fired as fast as he could pull the triggers, so fast that he could not aim with accuracy at the blurred figures which rushed toward him.

But the desperate hail of fire from his guns stopped the rush. The outlaws dropped back, and he saw one of them being carried. He slumped wearily, his heart pounding, his lungs pinching painfully because he had held his breath so long. With trembling fingers he reloaded the two guns and counted his cartridges.

Then he settled back and waited. Next time, they would get him.

Espy Norwood and Arch McCavitt rode side by side, Espy studying the soft tracks which they followed while Arch looked ahead, watching for sign of riders.

Espy swung down to check something on the ground. "Freshest sign we've seen, Arch," he said. "They're not far ahead of us now."

Arch frowned, jerking his head toward the west. "We better catch them pretty quick, or we're in for another night's camp, and a hungry one at that. It'll be dark in a little while."

Remounting, Espy nodded. "Yeah, and chances are Sam'll keep riding, like he did last night. Bet he knew we'd come after him. And he knew we'd figure that he was headed for Bowman's. So he didn't stay there long."

Arch grinned. "Well, I hope *I* never have to spend another night there. That place smells like somebody's hog pen."

The sun went down in a blaze of red and gold. Dusk closed over the two men like a fog.

Worriedly Arch asked, "You reckon we're ever going to find them?"

A sudden burst of gunfire exploded somewhere ahead of them. Espy glanced at Arch and caught the excitement in the redhead's eyes.

"We've just found them," Arch declared. They raked rowels along their horses' sides and sprang into a full run.

At the edge of the brush they reined up in a shower of sand. They stared hard into the darkness that gathered about the outlaw camp, trying to find where Sam was. Someone down there moved, and instantly a bullet sought after him.

"Sam's still in the game," Arch said in relief.

"Yeah, but we'd better get him out in a hurry. You ready?"

Arch nodded. "Ready."

Side by side they spurred out of the brush and into the outlaw camp. Arch's horse almost ran one man down. Caught by surprise, the rustlers put up no resistance for a moment.

"It's us, Sam," Espy called out. "Get up here behind me."

Sam wasted no time. Espy kicked his left foot free of the stirrup. Sam used the stirrup to swing up behind Espy's saddle. An outlaw came running, his gun blazing. Arch McCavitt cut him down.

"Let's go Arch!" Espy shouted.

In the space of five seconds they had ridden down into the camp and were spurring out again. The surprise was gone. Now Quirt Wolford was cursing and yelling for his men to rally.

"Get them! If they get away they'll hang us all!"

Guns began to talk. Bullets whispered over Espy's head. He bent low in the saddle and kept spurring. Then Quirt Wolford loomed ahead of him. Wolford's gun belched fire. Arch McCavitt jerked, then pitched forward in the saddle. Espy leveled one shot at Wolford and saw the man reel, grabbing his left arm, high against the shoulder.

Then Espy was busy grabbing at Arch, holding him in the saddle. His heart was one huge chunk of ice. "Hold on, cowboy," he gritted. "We're getting out of here."

Sam guided Espy to the point where he had left his horse. He mounted. Then the two of them held onto

Arch and kept spurring, trying to outrun the pursuing horsemen they could hear smashing through the brush behind them.

Quirt Wolford's arm burned as if a hot iron were driven into it. The blazing agony fed his fury.

"Get after them!" he bawled to his men who were swinging into their saddles. "Damn your cowardly souls, get them! Don't come back till they're all dead, do you hear?"

He choked on the dust that swirled from the horses' hoofs. He coughed it away and cursed the fire that ate at his arm.

Matt Ollinger caught him by his good shoulder and looked at the wound. "Looks bad, Quirt. You better do something about it. Or let me do it."

Ollinger led him into the dugout and lighted a lantern. He held a cloth to the torn flesh to slow the bleeding, lifting it occasionally to study the wound.

"Bullet's still in there, Quirt. We'll have to dig for it."

He reached upon a shelf and brought down a bottle. "Better take a good long drink, Quirt. This ain't gonna be fun."

Wolford gulped down some of the whisky, and Ollinger made him drink some more. Wolford's face, which had paled from shock, now began to flush with color again. He stretched out upon his bedroll on the dirt floor. Ollinger opened the long blade of his pocket knife and held it in the flame of the lantern until its edge began to glow. He let it cool, then began to probe at the wound.

Wolford cried out.

"Easy, Quirt," Ollinger said. "You better take another drink."

He went at it again. This time Wolford held on as

long as he could. Then his cry turned into a scream. The outlaw jumped up from the bedroll and shoved Ollinger aside in a roaring fury. Grabbing his bleeding arm, he lurched out the door and into the night.

Ollinger picked himself up from the dirt floor and hurried out after him. "Quirt," he said, "we've got to get that bullet out."

Wolford violently shook his head. He swayed drunkenly, half from the whisky and half from pain.

Ollinger argued. "You're liable to develop gangrene with that slug in there."

"No, I tell you!" Wolford's voice raged high and wild. "We'll leave it alone!"

After a while the men began straggling in. They shrank back from Wolford's blistering fury.

"It was just too dark, Quirt," Jake Claymore said.

Reeling as he walked, Wolford cursed them all, one at a time. Most especially he cursed Gid Bowman. When the rage was worked out of him, he sat down heavily.

The game was over, he knew that. It wouldn't be long now until the Figure 4 would sweep down here for vengeance. And Wolford's band wouldn't stand a chance against them. If only there were some way to stop the Figure 4 . . .

And suddenly in his desperation, he thought he saw the way. Matt Ollinger! And Espy Norwood's kid!

"Ollinger," he called out, "come over here. And Jake, you and Hatch too."

Matt Ollinger sauntered over. Claymore and Hatch followed him keeping their distance.

"Matt," Wolford said, "you're going to get Norwood's kid, all right, just the way we were talking about. Reckon that woman's in town by now?"

Ollinger nodded. "She ought to be."

"Then go find her. Tell her we'll have that youngster

for her by tomorrow night. After dark, you take her to the old Brewster shack just outside of town. We'll bring the kid.''

Wolford turned to Hatch and Claymore. ''It's up to you two to steal Norwood's kid and get him to Mobeetie by tomorrow night. You'll have to move plenty fast.''

Hatch stood defiantly. ''Not me, Quirt. I've had enough. You got me drunk and got me to stealing cattle. That's bad enough. But then murder, and now kidnaping. I won't have any part of it.''

Wolford slapped Hatch across the mouth with the back of his powerful hand. Hatch was big enough to put up a fight. But instead he backed off a step.

''Yes, you will,'' Wolford said. ''Getting our hands on that kid is the only thing that'll keep the Figure 4 off of us now. And you'll know where to find him. You'll help, Hatch. You'll help or I'll kill you!''

A few minutes later Hatch and Claymore rode out, toward the Figure 4. And Ollinger was on his way to Mobeetie.

Gripping his aching, burning arm, Wolford whirled upon his other men. ''Don't just stand around there. Mount up. We're getting out of the Panhandle. And we're taking the Arrowhead herd with us!''

XVII

Espy Norwood kept his horse close beside that of Arch McCavitt. His supporting arm was around Arch's shoulder, and Arch's weight was heavy against him. He held the horses still in a black pool of shadow, while Sam Kirk walked out into the starlight to listen, away from the horses and the creak of saddles. Presently Sam came back.

"I don't hear anything, Espy," he said. "I reckon they've turned back."

"It's a good thing. We've got to get Arch to town the quickest way we can."

Voice heavy with worry, Sam said. "I know a ranch west of Gid's place where we can get a wagon. But it's a long ride. Reckon Arch can make it?"

Espy shook his head. His throat was so tight it hurt him. "We've got to try. I've stopped his bleeding, but he's in a bad way."

Espy sighted on the stars, and they rode out. They tried a jog trot but had to give it up. It was too hard on Arch. So they settled down to a walk, slow as it was. Espy held Arch a while, then Sam took a turn.

After an hour of riding in silence, Espy said, "Sam, there's a lot here that I don't know. And I think it's time somebody told me."

Sam was a long while in answering. "Yes, Espy, I suppose so. After all this, you're going to find out anyway. I'd rather you found out from me, so you'll know just the way everything was.

"Frank Bowman was a good man, Espy. I want you to know that right at the start. He did what he did because he thought he was justified. When he found out he was wrong, it was too late for him to back out.

"He was a farsighted man, Mr. Frank was. The Figure 4 had always been a profitable outfit. But he could see another day coming. He knew the free range wasn't going to last many more years. Settlers were already beginning to show up, buying state land they hadn't ever seen and coming to take it, even if it was in the middle of somebody's ranch.

"Some outfits fought them. But not Mr. Frank. The way he saw it, they had the deeds and the land was theirs. So instead of fighting, he tried to buy up or lease up the land he had built the Figure 4 on. He had just as well have butted his head against an adobe wall.

"Turned out the land certificates were in the hands of a bunch of speculators in Austin. They found that Mr. Frank had a big investment in improvements already and wanted the place mighty bad. So they shoved the price up sky-high. He just couldn't go it."

Espy nodded. He could understand that. He knew that Texas was one of the most unusual of all the states in that it owned all its land. In most states the land originally belonged to the federal government. But Texas, bargaining as an independent republic, had retained title to its land. Later, as a young state, it had made good use of land in place of currency. Certificates for millions of acres floated around all over the state. And many of the holders had never even seen their own land.

Sam said, "Mr. Frank got to looking around and found a man who had certificates on land west of here. Not as good as the Figure 4, mind you, and not near as much of it. But it was a nice place, anyway. Mr. Frank paid him all he could on it and promised him the rest soon.

"So, to raise the rest of the money he needed, he sold a half interest in the Figure 4 operation to the syndicate you're working for. He knew it wouldn't be many years before he'd have to give up the Figure 4 range anyway, so he didn't figure the partnership could last too long. He let the syndicate write in some mighty strong terms, just so he could get the money.

"That's the reason the syndicate had the right to name its own manager after he died. It just never entered Mr. Frank's head that he wouldn't outlive the partnership."

Sam scowled. "Well, Espy, you know the history of the syndicate, and the kind of trash they sent out here. Drunkards and arrogant asses that somebody wanted to get rid of for a while. First thing we knew they were running the place to suit themselves, or at least were trying to. Mr. Frank was a patient man, and he stood it a long time. But finally he turned bitter about it too.

"Worst thing was that to show how important they were, they started accusing him of first one thing, then another. They'd get peeved over some little thing and start threatening to sue him, to take over his share of the partnership. He was scared, Espy. He was afraid they could do it, if the thing ever went to a high court. He didn't think a little man like him could whip a big outfit like the syndicate.

"Then his brother Gid got to working on him. 'Bite them before they bite you,' he kept telling Mr. Frank. 'They're going to get you sooner or later. You better take all you can from them before they do.'

"Mr. Frank was no thief, Espy. But it looked to him like the syndicate was out to swindle him. How was he to know that these blowhards didn't speak for the whole bunch?

"In self-protection he let Gid take a few Figure 4 cattle, change the brands over into an Arrowhead, and drive them to the new ranch farther west. Somehow or other Quirt Wolford threw in with Gid. They didn't stop with a few cattle, they took a lot. And a good many of them never got to Mr. Frank's other ranch.

"I started missing cattle. One day a couple of the boys and I trailed a bunch and ran into Wolford and some of his men. One of the Figure 4 punchers got shot in the arm. After that, Mr. Frank told me what he'd done.

"I tried to talk to him, to make him see what he was getting into. But by this time the thing was plumb out of hand. Mr. Frank saw he'd done wrong. But it was like starting a big rock to rolling down a hill and not being able to stop it. He couldn't make Wolford and Gid quit. They'd gotten the taste, and they liked it too well. Mr. Frank was in too deep himself to go to the law. There was only one way. But Gid Bowman was his brother, and Mr. Frank wouldn't do it.

"So the thing went on, and got worse all the time. Some of the cattle got to the Arrowhead, but a lot of them didn't. Some of the cowboys began to figure it out. They didn't want to get mixed up in it, so they started leaving. That's why Mr. Frank took to hiring the slowest, sorriest men that came around. He didn't think they were apt to get wise.

"It was showing up in the cattle counts, bad. So I started doctoring up the tallies to help Mr. Frank, hoping all the time that something would happen, and we could straighten out. Before long I had myself stuck to it and couldn't turn aloose.

"Mr. Frank's health wasn't any too good anyway. The worry just about finished him. Then the syndicate sent Geoffrey Spence out here. He was as different from the others as daylight from dark. And smart . . .

He began adding things up for himself. So one day Mr.
Frank squared his shoulders and told him the whole
story, with me sitting there listening.

"But Quirt Wolford got his hands on the message
Spence sent to headquarters in Kansas City. A couple
of days later, Spence was killed in a 'hunting accident.'

"Mr. Frank knew it was murder. It was more than he
could take. His heart just gave out on him."

Sam Kirk's voice was taut with hatred. "Quirt Wolford killed him, Espy. He killed Frank Bowman just as
sure as he killed Spence and Cotton.

"After Mr. Frank was buried, I sat down and wrote a
letter to the syndicate. I told them the story. Three
nights later, Quirt Wolford brought it back. He had
stolen it out of the post office, the way he was stealing
any other Figure 4 mail that looked important—the
way he'd gotten his hands on Spence's report.

"Wolford warned me not to try anything like that
again. He said that if the syndicate caught up with him,
he'd implicate me in Spence's murder. It wouldn't be
hard to do, because I'd been with Spence a good part of
the day he was killed. And what I had done to the tallies
would make it look even worse.

"Nobody else knew the story, nobody but Arch
McCavitt. he'd figured most of it out, and I'd admitted
the rest to him. Not even Mary Bowman had any idea
what had been taking place the last three years. So I was
stuck, Espy.

"Then you came along. The first time I saw you, I
knew you were the kind of man who wouldn't stop
digging till you had the truth. That's why I tried to
block you. Now you know it all. You can do what you
want to about it."

Espy nodded grimly. "I'm glad you told me, Sam. It
ties up a lot of loose strings that've been dangling. And

whatever happens now, I'll see that you're in the clear.''

He was thinking of one thing in particular, a letter he had found in Gid Bowman's dugout, and his resulting accusation of Mary Bowman. He had been wrong, he could see that now.

But Sam's story wasn't going to help Colonel Judkins's position against the syndicate directors when they got here. If anything, it would make the situation even more hopeless. They would break the colonel. There wouldn't be a thing Espy could do to help him.

When daylight came and they struck a trail that was familiar to Sam, they eased Arch to the ground under the shade of a chinaberry. Sam loped ahead. Much later he came back in a wagon, his horse tied on behind. A cowboy from the other ranch was with him.

Arch had lapsed into complete unconsciousness, his breathing labored. Espy and Sam carefully placed him on a mattress that had been put in the back of the wagon. Re-examining Arch's wound, Espy said, "What do you think Quirt Wolford will do now, Sam? He'll know it won't be long till we'll be back to get him.''

Worriedly Sam said, "I expect he'll try to get out of the country. And knowing Wolford, I don't think he'll go out empty-handed.''

"What do you mean?''

"I mean that it's not extra far from the Arrowhead to the New Mexico line. Wolford's got a greedy streak in him a foot wide. Those cattle in the Arrowhead brand belong to Mary and the syndicate. But I'd bet you a hundred dollars Wolford tries to take them with him, if he thinks he's got any chance at all.''

Espy rubbed the back of his neck It made sense. "Then you go back to the ranch, Sam. Round up the

men. I can get Arch to Mobeetie with your friend's
help.

"Get the Figure 4 outfit to town as quick as you can,
and I'll go with you from there. If Wolford tries to take
the Arrowhead herd, we'll stop him. And this time, he
won't get away."

Margaret Tellison sat in her hotel room, nervously
fanning herself with a folded sheet of paper and wishing
it weren't so miserably hot. Her window was up, but
she didn't dare sit near it. The door was closed and the
lock bar fitted firmly in place.

Her heartbeat still quickened every time she remembered the narrow escape she had had this morning. For
two days she had stayed close to her hotel room,
answering to the name of Jones and awaiting some
word from that disreputable man, Ollinger. This morning, unable to hold herself in any longer, she had gone
out for a stroll. And on the plank sidewalk in front of a
long frame saloon building, she had almost come face
to face with Espy Norwood.

She had seen him just in time, helping lift an unconscious man out of a wagon and carry him inside. Margaret Tellison had shrunk back into the recessed doorway of an adobe building and waited there with ashen
face, her heart driving like a pump handle. Only when
Espy no longer was in sight did she realize she was in
the entrance of a saloon, and half a dozen men were
staring. She had whirled around, hurried back to her
room, and locked herself in.

Later, when someone had knocked on her door, she
had shrunk against the wall, afraid to answer, mortally
fearful that it was Espy Norwood, that he had seen her
after all.

Only when Matt Ollinger called his name had she
opened the door.

"Be ready when dark comes," he told her. "A friend of mine will bring the boy."

Ollinger had hesitated a moment before adding, 'And by the way, don't say anything about your agreement with me, about the money you're to pay me. I'd rather my friend didn't know our arrangements."

The hotel manager had told her about Espy Norwood and Arch McCavitt later, when he brought her meal to her room.

"Arch is laid up in the back room of his place," the gray-mustached man said worriedly. "Can't tell yet whether he's going to pull through or not. Looks mighty bad. Doctor told me he hasn't been conscious since Norwood brought him in."

Margaret remembered Arch McCavitt from a long time ago. A red-haired cowboy, wild, uncouth. She had always known he would come to no good end.

A sudden thought struck her and brought a clutch of fear to her throat. What if it hadn't been Arch? What if Espy had been shot instead?

When darkness came, she was pacing the floor of the tiny room, excitement prickling her skin like needles. Her imagination ran wild. What if something went wrong? What if they let something happen to Kenny, those impossible ruffians? What if Espy caught up with her before she could get Kenny back to the protection of Kansas City?

Her nerves stretched taut as a fiddlestring. Frightened tears were burning her eyes when Ollinger's knock finally sounded on the wooden door.

"Ready, Mrs. Tellison?"

He had rented a buggy in the name of Mrs. Jones, and it was waiting in back of the hotel. Silently he flipped the reins, and they pulled away into the night. The nearness of this rough man, sitting close beside her on the buggy seat, set her heart to beating in fear. She shrank away from the smell of sweat and tobacco which clung heavily to him. She hoped to heaven that never again would she be forced to deal with men of this kind.

It took half an hour to reach the shack. Before they got there, Ollinger stopped the team. "I'll take my money now, before we go on in."

Stiffly she said, "The agreement was that I pay you when I get Kenny."

"He's there. And you'll pay me now!"

She hesitated, but her pounding heart got the best of her. The money was rolled and tied in her purse. He hefted it, then shoved it in his pocket without counting it. "It'd better be all there," he said. "Remember, I know where *you* live."

Yellow lamplight reached out from the shack's tiny windows. Ollinger helped her down. In her excitement she hurried to the shack and reached for the door. Ollinger grabbed her arm and jerked her back.

"You want to get shot? We better sing out before we start in there."

He called, "It's me . . . Ollinger!" The door swung inward.

Margaret rushed inside, Kenny's eyes widened, then he hurried into her arms. "Aunt Margaret," he cried, "what're you doing here?"

She hugged him tightly, then held him off for a look. "You poor darling. You've been frightened to death."

He drew back. "No, I'm not. I'm not scared, not a bit." His voice was a little wavery, but he was putting up a game show. "Are you going to take me back to Daddy?"

The eagerness of his question set Margaret aback. She didn't know quite what to say. It hadn't once entered her mind that he might want to go back to his father.

She looked for the first time at the men around her.

Two had the appearance of common cowboys. But the third one made her take an involuntary step backward. She tried hard to keep the blood from draining out of her face. He was big and broad-shouldered, with a black beard and fevered black eyes. His left sleeve was torn away and the arm bound tightly by a dirty cloth, which had been soaked through with blood, now dried a wine red and turned to hard crust.

She feared him instinctively, the same way she knew and feared a mean dog even before it showed its teeth.

His burning eyes glared at her. He swayed drunkenly. But he wasn't drunk. He was sick.

His voice was drawn up tightly, as if in pain. "You've got your boy, Mrs. Tellison. Now how about the money?"

She saw the sudden worry waft into Ollinger's washed-out eyes.

"I don't know what you mean," she told Quirt Wolford.

He snarled, "You take me for a fool, woman? You think I'm stupid enough to believe a man like Matt Ollinger would agree to kidnap this boy for you just because he hates Espy Norwood. How much have you paid him?"

Hesitantly she said, "Five hundred dollars."

"Give it to me, Matt."

Ollinger reached for his gun. But sick though he was, Wolford beat him. Ollinger let his gun slip back into the holster, his black-whiskered face a shade whiter.

"I said give it to me, Matt."

Smoldering, Ollinger pulled out the roll. "Take it, Jake," Wolford ordered. "Count it."

Jake Claymore quickly ran through it. "It's all here."

"Give half of it back to Ollinger."

Scowling, Matt Ollinger snatched his share.

Wolford's lips formed a hard smile. "Next time, Matt Ollinger, you'll not try to cheat me. You thought we'd take the risk and you'd take the money. They don't do that to Quirt Wolford. Not but once."

Wolford's feverish eyes flicked back to Margaret Tellison. "How much more you got in that purse?"

Defensively she held it tight against her bosom.

"Get it, Jake." Claymore wrested it from her hands, took the remaining money out of it, and thrust the empty purse back at her.

Choking down her rage, she drew Kenny to her. But he pulled away, his eyes accusing her. "Did you do what the man said, Aunt Margaret? Did you have them steal me away from my daddy?"

The hurt in his voice brought burning tears to her eyes. "Kenny, *I* didn't steal you—your father did. He stole you from me."

The boy pulled away from her. "I want to go back to him."

"Kenny, I'm taking you to Kansas City."

"No! I don't want to go back there. I want to go to Daddy."

Quirt Wolford made a signal, and Jake Claymore caught hold of the boy.

Wolford said roughly, "He's not going anywhere with you, and he's not going to his dad either. He's going with *us.*"

She raised her hands to her face, wanting to cry out but unable to do it.

"You take a message to Espy Norwood for me," Wolford said. "Tell him we've got his boy. And tell him that if he wants to see this kid alive again, he'd better leave us alone. Tell him we're getting out of Texas and we're taking the Arrowhead herd with us. If he makes a move to stop us, this kid'll die!"

Margaret Tellison fell to her knees, sobbing uncontrollably. She reached out a hand toward Kenny and touched nothing.

Wolford looked contemptuously at Matt Ollinger. "You coming with us?"

The outlaw hesitated a moment, his pale eyes ruefully observing the empty purse that lay open at his feet. "Yeah," he gritted. "Guess I'd just as well."

They walked out into the darkness, and in a moment the hoofbeats had faded out of hearing. The only sound left was the desperate sobbing of the woman who lay face down upon the floor.

XVIII

ESPY'S SLEEPLESS eyes burned as if there were sand in them. He had dozed a little, off and on through the day, but that was all the sleep he had had. Now, under the restful glow of lamplight, he leaned his straight chair backward on two legs, resting his head wearily against the flowered wallpaper.

The girl Lilybelle had hardly moved from her chair at Arch's bedside. When Arch showed signs of stirring, she arose quickly, hopefully, tenderly touching his face or his hand with her fingers. And when Arch lapsed back into stillness, she would slowly sink down again, the silent tears glistening on her cheeks.

No paint and powder now hid the grave beauty of her face. Her dress was a plain, simple one. A small gold cross hung over her breast. Several times Espy had seen her clutch the cross, her head bowed, her eyes closed.

Heavyhearted, Espy closed his own eyes. He tried to doze, bending his head forward so that his stubbled chin almost touched his chest. Through his mind ran tortured thoughts of Arch McCavitt, and Quirt Wolford, of Mary Bowman, who must now learn that her father had been stealing his own partnership cattle, of Colonel Judkins, who soon was to lose everything he owned. Any day now, that attorney Slagel was due here with some of the syndicate directors. The fur was about to fly.

Espy dozed. A hard, urgent rapping on the door jerked him upright, blinking in sleepy-eyed surprise.

"Espy!" a woman cried. Espy hurried to the door, thinking of Mary Bowman. But it wasn't Mary Bowman. He stepped back, astonished.

Margaret Tellison's hair was in disarray, her eyes red from crying, her lips pinched and pale. "Espy," she sobbed, "those horrible men—they've taken Kenny."

For a moment he was speechless, completely dumfounded by her presence here. "What men, Margaret?"

She broke hysterically. "They'll kill him, they'll kill him!"

In sudden desperation Espy grabbed her shoulders and shook her violently. *"Who,* Margaret? Who's got Kenny?"

Somehow she managed to blurt out the whole story. A helpless weakness washed through Espy. He sank into the chair, his head in his hands.

"Why did you do it, Margaret?" he asked, hardly above a whisper. "Do you hate me so much?"

He was totally unprepared for what she did then. She knelt before him and took his hands. "No, Espy. I don't hate you. I *never* hated you. I've loved you almost since the first time we met."

He stared at her, not able to believe. Her voice was set hard in an effort to keep it from breaking.

"I tried to fight myself, Espy, and when I couldn't do that, I fought you. Ever since I've been old enough to think for myself, I had my mind made up. I was sick of small-town life, of small-town poverty. I was going to marry a man who could take me away from that. I had it all planned.

"Then you came along. I did everything I could to rid myself of my love for you. It didn't work, not even after Jeannie married you. I thought after I married Edgar Tellison it would be different. But it wasn't, Espy. I was still in love with you.

"That's why I wanted Kenny, I guess. If I couldn't have you, then I wanted your son. Can't you see, Espy? Can't you understand how it was?"

Her shoulders shook, and she bowed her head so he could not see her face. "Espy, can you ever forgive me?"

He pulled his hands away and turned his back. For a long time he stood there thinking, his face heavy with despair. Finally he turned back and looked down at her. "I forgive you, Margaret. But I want you to leave. I never want to see you again."

He added then, "I'm sorry for you, Margaret."

She begged, "Is sympathy all you feel for me, Espy?"

He nodded. "That's all. That's all there'll ever be."

She stood up slowly, her back set rigid in resignation. "Good-bye, Espy."

"Good-bye," he told her. And she was gone.

In black misery, he sank into his chair. Lilybelle had watched and listened without a word. Now she arose and walked to him. With a compassionate hand on his shoulder, she said, "Your son?"

He nodded, unable to speak.

Her voice was bitter as she looked toward Arch. "So Quirt Wolford gets away. But someday, somewhere, I may see him again. And if I do, Espy, I promise you I'll *kill* him!"

Unable to bear the cramped little room, Espy shoved through the door and walked out into the saloon itself. There was little trade tonight, and what customers were there kept their voices subdued. Everyone knew about Arch.

Espy pulled out a chair and sat down at a table alone. With his knotted fist he struck the tabletop so hard that the sardine-can ash tray bounced off and clattered on the floor.

He sat there a while, not seeing, not hearing. Then he signaled the bartender. "Whisky," he said.

The strong smell of it pinched his face as he poured the tall glass half full. Something within him cried out a warning. But one wouldn't hurt him. He *had* to have something.

He took it all in one long gulp and strained for breath as its fire burned down his throat. He felt the warmth of it spread through his body and into his brain. The first he'd had in more than a year. The terrible craving began to eat at him. He wanted more. The voice within cried out again, and yet another time. But Espy Norwood no longer heard. He never stopped until the bottle was empty, and he slumped senseless upon the table.

A strong hand shook his shoulder. He stirred resentfully, his head exploding in pain, his eyes aching unmercifully against the bright glare of daylight. He shut them tightly.

"Espy," a girl's voice said. "Espy, come out of it."

He turned over and almost fell to the floor. He realized dully that he was lying on a steel cot. He let his feet fall heavily over the side. He sat up on the edge of the cot, both hands pressed hard against his head. He could hear Mary Bowman's voice, but was still unable to see her.

"Espy, please, get hold of yourself."

When finally he could see again, he found that he was in Arch's room. Somebody had set up a folding steel cot and placed him upon it. Lilybelle still sat where she had been. Her face was drawn and her eyes ringed with gray. She still hadn't slept. And Arch hadn't awakened.

Mary Bowman stood in front of Espy, her hand on his shoulder. Sam Kirk waited behind her.

"Espy," Mary insisted, "you've got to come

around. The Figure 4 directors got to town last night. The man Slagel has heard everything. He's bringing them here right now.''

Espy heard the words, but he had a hard time getting them through his head. "Mary," he said, "when did you get here?"

"We got in a little bit ago. We rode through the night. The whole Figure 4 is here."

Espy shook his head. It seemed to be getting clearer. He looked past Mary, to Sam. "Sam, did you tell her?"

Mary answered for him. Tight-lipped, she said, "Yes, Espy, he told me everything. Now, get up, quickly. You've got to get straightened out before Slagel gets here."

Espy stood up uncertainly. The room reeled about him. His head was still splitting. Mary caught hold of him, steadying him.

"I'm sorry, Mary," he said. Shame kindled hotly within him. "I've made a big fool of myself. For more than a year, I held myself back. And last night I just let everything go."

She smiled tightly, her voice sympathetic. "I understand, Espy. You don't have to apologize to me."

"I won't ever do it again, Mary," he insisted. "I promise you."

"I'm glad Espy. But hurry. You've got to get cleaned up."

A water pitcher and washbasin sat on a small stand against the wall. Espy poured the basin full of water, glancing at himself in the mirror above the stand. He looked like a bear coming out of hibernation, his hair atangle, his eyes still red, his face whiskery.

The cold water against his face braced him some, but he was still wobbly on his feet. He ran a comb through his tangled hair, wincing at the way it pulled.

He heard a commotion outside the room, in the saloon, and he heard a voice say, "He's in here, gentlemen."

Opening the door, Espy walked unsteadily out into the saloon. The tall, spidery lawyer confronted him triumphantly. Slagel turned back to the half dozen men who accompanied him.

"There, gentlemen. Now you see the kind of man to whom Colonel Judkins has entrusted our huge investment."

He shook his cane in Espy's face. "You're a disgrace, Norwood. Is it any wonder that with men like you running our affairs out here, Colonel Judkins has allowed our partner to steal us blind?"

Espy stiffened, a ripple of heat working under his skin.

Slagel went on. "A drunken lout. That's the kind of man you sent out here, Colonel."

Espy's chin dropped. Colonel Judkins was here! The old man slowly stepped out from among the directors. He stared unbelievingly at Espy, his dark brown eyes pinched with pain, his weathered face long and grave.

Voice bitter with disappointment, he said, "Espy, I wish I hadn't come."

The colonel might have believed him. But Slagel never gave him time to answer.

"Perhaps you sent this kind of man here on purpose, Colonel. Perhaps you were stealing from us just the way Frank Bowman was."

Espy exploded. His fist came up like a rock from a slingshot. Slagel's head jerked violently. The lawyer reeled backward, striking a table and knocking it over, sprawling ignominiously on the floor. He lay there a minute, shaking his head, half senseless.

Espy saw the color leave the colonel's face. Suddenly Judkins was an old, old man, the spirit and the will completely gone. The colonel sank into a handy chair, his face a gray mask of hopelessness.

This finished it. He was ruined now.

Espy's shoulders slumped. Shame spilled over him. His head hanging, he said, "I'm sorry, sir."

Judkins answered weakly, "No need to apologize, Espy. *I'm* the one at fault, not you. You didn't want the job, and I all but forced it on you. I'm the one who should've known better."

The half dozen directors had all stood in shocked silence, not one of them speaking. Mary Bowman suddenly spoke up, her voice strong and determined.

"Just a moment, gentlemen," she said, "before you condemn Espy Norwood, or Colonel Judkins. Neither of them has done any wrong, and Slagel knows it. He has lied to you.

"Yes, you've lost cattle, a lot of cattle. I won't deny that. But I promise you that I'll make up your losses.

"I don't expect any of you gentlemen to understand what made my father do what he did. But *I* understand, and I know he was wrong. I don't want anything that doesn't belong to me. We'll round up the Figure 4 cattle. If there aren't as many left as the syndicate is entitled to, I'll make it up out of the Arrowhead herd. You won't lose a thing, gentlemen. That's a promise."

Staring at the girl, Espy felt the stir of admiration, of deepest pride. When this was over, she wouldn't have enough cattle left to stock a nester spread. She must know that. And yet, to save him, and to save Colonel Judkins, she was giving up all she owned.

The colonel looked at her in disbelief, his square beard trembling. One of the directors grinned. "By Jove, gentlemen, I'm for it."

Another chimed in, an American voice. "Sounds square to me."

Espy breathed easier, and some of the weight slid from his shoulders. But a chilling thought came back to him. Sam Kirk voiced it for him.

"There won't be any Arrowhead herd, Mary, if we don't stop Quirt Wolford. And we can't do that. He has Kenny Norwood in his hands."

Espy Norwood felt all eyes turn toward him. And now came the bitterest decision he had ever made in his life. He walked to the open door and looked out upon the dirt street of Mobeetie. He thought of Frank and Mary Bowman, of Geoffrey Spence, of Cotton Dulaney and Arch McCavitt—of all those who had suffered because of Quirt Wolford. Most of all he thought of Kenny.

Three men had already died for the Figure 4. Another lay in the back room there, hovering on the dark brink between life and death. Were it his own life in the balance, Espy would know what to do. But it *wasn't* his life.

Espy shut his eyes tight, trying to hold back the burning in them.

The answer came to him, plain and inescapable. Kenny was yet a boy, but he was game. His fight with Joe Kirk had been ample proof of that. Old Jess Cooley had told Espy the story. In only a few years Kenny would be a man. And were he a man, what would be his decision?

Espy knew, for it would be the same as his own.

He turned back toward the waiting group, his eyes bleak.

"If we're going to catch Wolford, we'd better be a'riding."

XIX

A LAZY film of dust followed the strung-out Arrowhead herd, slowly dissolving in the easy warmth of a summer wind. The pace was brisk, for Quirt Wolford's men were pushing hard, yelling, swinging their ropes, crowding, shoving.

And up and down both sides of the herd, Quirt Wolford rode endlessly, shouting and cursing, punishing his horse, punishing his men, punishing himself.

The small calves and the older cows had dropped back farther and farther until now they were in the drags.

Gid Bowman rode there, heavy and lifeless in his saddle. Claude Hatch was there, too, with the boy Kenny Norwood, shoving the tail end of the herd. Face masked by sweat-streaked dust, Hatch rode out to meet Wolford.

"Quirt," he protested, "we're driving too fast. Calves back here can't keep up."

Wolford scowled at him. His left arm hung limp. His black eyes were ablaze with fever. Half the time he stayed in the saddle only because of the tight grip his right hand held on the horn. He swayed, his face slack in a sick, pasty pallor.

"Leave them, then," he growled. "We got no time to worry about the slow ones."

He jerked his square chin toward Bowman and the kid. "Is Gid still drinking back there?"

Hatch nodded. Wolford said something under his

breath, then, ''Tell him, by God, that if he gets too drunk to ride, we'll just leave him afoot. He's been on that bottle ever since they shot up our camp.

''Now keep these drags moving, Hatch. I'll shoot the man who lags!''

Cruelly he jerked his horse around and headed once more toward the point to keep them moving.

About midway, Matt Ollinger reined in his horse a moment, catching his breah and looking back toward the dusty drags. He saw Wolford coming, and hatred crept into Ollinger's dust-burned eyes. He asked himself why he had stayed. But he knew. Wolford was riding for a fall. And maybe Ollinger could pick up the pieces.

They had made a swift drag over the Arrowhead range. There hadn't been time enough or men enough for a thorough sweep. But they had gotten away with a big part of the herd. He guessed there were a thousand head or so here.

Wolford furiously reined in beside him. ''Keep moving, Ollinger. Nobody's slacking up on this drive. Nobody!''

Ollinger's pale eyes narrowed dangerously. ''Hold on, Wolford. You don't talk to me like that. Nobody does. I came along because I wanted to. I don't take orders, I do what I choose.''

Wolford's right hand slid off the saddle horn and onto the butt of his gun. ''You'll do as I say! Shove cattle or I'll shoot you right where you stand!''

Ollinger bristled, but he could see the rattlesnake fury behind Wolford's black eyes. He weighed his chances and knew they were slim.

Ollinger rode off, yelling at some lagging cows, forcing them to break into a stiff trot. Wolford stayed back, too cagey even in his fever to ride ahead and risk a bullet in his back.

Ollinger's cheeks were rigid. A storm brewed in his sky-pale eyes. When he was far enough ahead of Wolford, he dropped back to the man behind him, a gangling, scar faced outlaw they all called Mose.

Jerking his head Wolford's way, Ollinger said, "He been chewing on you too?"

Mose scowled, deepening the long scar that ran down his cheek. "Who ain't he been chewing on?"

"How long are we going to take it, Mose?"

The tall rider's eyebrows lifted. "What're you getting at?"

Ollinger said, "He's going crazy with pain and fever. That bullet's still in his arm, and it's going to kill him. But he's going to kill some of us first, the way he's going. Are we just going to wait around for it to happen?"

Mose frowned. "I don't know what we can do about it."

"We'll wait for our chance and get his guns. Then we can set him afoot and take the herd for ourselves."

"That's pretty rank, Ollinger."

"Is it any worse than he deserves, Mose? Haven't you had a bellyful of him cursing you and driving you, and taking a lion's share of everything? And if it's a fight you're a-scared of, don't be. In his shape, without his gun, he'll be like a rattler with his fangs pulled out."

Mose pondered a moment. "Reckon you're right, Ollinger. He's had it coming. Holler when you're ready."

Ollinger rode on ahead, to talk to the next man, and start the word passing around the herd.

Wolford rode toward the drags again. The smell of his horse's sweat was strong and sour. The animal was giving out, and it was a long way to the New Mexico line, even yet. Wolford hunched over the horn, his arm throbbing unmercifully, a deep throbbing agony that reached all the way to his brain. A swimmy red haze was beginning to obscure his sight.

He pulled up beside Claude Hatch and the kid. "Get off that horse, button. I'm taking it."

Defiantly Kenny sat still. Wolford caught his thin shoulder and hurled him down. Laboriously Wolford eased to the ground. Kenny Norwood had gotten up and was dusting off his clothes. He scooped up a rock and hurled it at Wolford. The outlaw twisted away from it, but it struck his wounded arm. He cried out against the blinding surge of pain. He grabbed the boy and flung him to the ground again.

Claude Hatch dismounted and caught the boy. He shoved Kenny behind him. "That's enough, Quirt. He's just a kid."

His voice trembled with anger. Ever since last night, he had watched in silent rage while Wolford mishandled the boy, flinging him around, striking him, cursing him. Now it was time to stop being silent.

Wolford calmed a little. "His horse is fresher. I want him. Change my saddle over, Hatch. The kid can take my horse. And he'd better make him keep up."

Hatch changed the saddles. The herd was drifting on away, with Bowman slacked drunkenly behind the drags.

Worriedly Hatch asked, "What do you figure on doing with the kid, Quirt, when we get to safety?"

"What do you care?" was Wolford's bitter reply. "You hate Espy Norwood same as the rest of us do."

Fear weakened Hatch's voice. "That don't call for killing kids."

"I won't leave him to talk. You don't have to watch it, Hatch. Now get back to the herd, and make that kid work."

Wolford struggled back into the saddle, his face purpling with pain.

Hatch flung the boy's saddle onto Wolford's tired mount, watching in fear and black hatred as the big outlaw rode away. Wolford's back made a broad target. For a moment Hatch's hand rested on his gun. It would be easy, from here. He even went so far as to draw the gun half out of the holster. But his hand shook, and his heart rose high in his throat. He dropped the gun back where it belonged, cursing himself for a coward.

When the horse was saddled, Hatch looked down at the boy. For several hours a half-formed idea had been running through his desperate mind. Now was the time, if he was ever going to do it.

"Wolford aims to kill you, boy," he said bluntly. "Our only chance is to run. It's a poor chance, but the only one we've got. Are you game?"

His tanning face drawn up grimly, Kenny nodded. "I'm game."

Wolford had disappeared over a rise. Bowman had his bottle lifted high. Half a dozen cows had dropped back behind the drunken man. He hadn't seen them. He wasn't seeing anything.

"Let's go," Hatch said.

They spurred into a lope, heading straight east. A little to the right ran a green, brushy draw. Hatch pulled toward it, hoping it would hide them, hoping desperately that no one would see them riding away.

Gaining the safety of the draw, he pulled up a moment and looked back. No one was coming. Maybe they could get a long start before they were missed.

"We're going to have to push, Kenny. I don't know how long your horse will hold out, but we'll have to run him for all he's got. And when he's gone, we'll double up on mine. Let's ride."

They spurred out again, both too busy now to be looking back.

Wolford never missed them until he made another inspection of the drags. He jerked erect in the saddle as he realized that Gid Bowman was alone.

Cursing darkly, he spurred to Bowman's side. "Where's Hatch?" he demanded. "Where's that kid?"

Reeking of whisky, Bowman stared at him bleary-eyed. He mumbled something unintelligible and hunched lower in the saddle.

Wolford looked back to the cattle that had strung out behind the sodden ranchman. The rest of the story was glaringly clear.

A choking rage swept Quirt Wolford. His right hand moved with a blur. The first shot rocked Gid Bowman back. The second knocked him spinning from the saddle. Bowman's horse squealed in terror and whirled away, loping pell-mell around the herd, reins trailing. Wolford leaned over Bowman's body and emptied his gun in a blind red spasm of fury.

The sudden violence drew the other men quickly. They gathered in a circle around Wolford, their eyes first on him, then on the torn body of Gid Bowman, whose lifeless fingers still choked the neck of a bottle while the last of the red liquid drained out and was swallowed up by the thirsty sand.

"Ollinger! Mose!" Wolford shouted. "He let Hatch and the kid get away. Go after them! Bring them back!"

Ollinger glanced over the other men and saw grim agreement in their eyes. Now was the time.

"No, Quirt," he answered. "You've given your last order."

Wolford's face was ablaze. He brought up the gun.

But it was empty. He stared unbelievingly at his riders who now ringed him, faces sullen and defiant.

"What is this?" he demanded. "What does this mean?"

Ollinger answered curtly. "It means you're through, Quirt. We're taking your guns and we're taking your herd!"

Realization was a long time soaking in. And when it did, Wolford slumped, a sick man, a desperate man.

"But why? Why?"

"Because you're not a man anymore, you're a hydrophobia wolf. That wounded arm has driven you out of your head, and we've had to suffer for it. But now it's just you, Quirt. We're going on without you."

Ollinger was in favor of leaving him afoot and helpless, to die on the prairie. But a couple of the men held out against that.

"All right, then," Ollinger said finally, "we'll let you keep your horse. But no guns. And stay away from us. If you show up near the herd, we'll kill you on sight!"

So Quirt Wolford was cast adrift. He rode off alone, hunched low over his saddle horn, his swollen, throbbing arm hanging useless at his side.

"He won't last a day," somebody said.

Now Matt Ollinger was the boss, and he was quick to show it. "Wolford was right about one thing," he said. "Without that boy for a hostage, we haven't got a chance. You men keep the herd moving, fast. Mose, you go with me. We're going to get that kid!"

Kenny Norwood's horse was flagging fast. He'd gotten a good run out of him that first mile. But now he was slowing down.

"Keep him coming, kid," Claude Hatch said desperately. "We've got to make all the miles we can."

A rider can sense when an animal beneath him has to labor harder and harder to keep up his speed.

Kenny got another mile out of him. But now it was over.

Claude Hatch got down and unsaddled the worn-out animal. Slipping the bridle off and dropping it to the ground, he waited for the horse to move. It didn't. It stood heaving, the sweat dripping.

Hatch mounted first, then gave Kenny a lift up behind the saddle. They set out again at a slower pace, saving strength.

They had gained another three or four miles when Kenny looked over his shoulder. "They're coming," he shouted. "Two of them."

Hatch glanced back once to see how much of a lead he had. Then he touched spurs to his sorrel and called up the speed he had saved. With no stirrups, Kenny began to bounce. He hugged up against Hatch and held onto him like a burr. Hatch kept his spurs raking. For a long time he maintained the lead. But slowly he began to lose it. The two riders were catching up.

Desperately he looked for some sign of help, a house or a shack or a dugout. But he saw none, and he knew there wouldn't be one. There was nothing to do but run as long as he could, then stop and fight.

Ahead of them, cradled between a double row of cottonwoods and cedar, he saw a crooked creek bed. He made for it, spurring hard. When he reached it, he pulled to a quick stop, swung his right leg over the horse's neck, and dropped off on the left side. He lifted Kenny forward into the saddle.

"Move out, kid," he said quickly. "Head for Mobeetie. Follow the creek till you're out of sight. It's you they want, and maybe I can fool them here for a while."

Before Kenny could say a word, Hatch slapped the

horse across the rump and sent him running.

Hatch bellied down behind a flood-cut bank, gun in hand. He took off his gunbelt and laid it out beside him, where he could reach the cartridges easier. When the riders were two hundred yards away, he fired the first shot. That would slow them down. They would be a long time closing in.

Not one hour had passed since he had joined Quirt Wolford that he had not cursed himself for a fool, and flinched under the cruel whip of conscience. The big dreams he had dreamed were gone like the smoke from yesterday's fire. There had been a time, once, when he might have made them a reality. But not now. He had smashed them. No one else could be blamed for it, really. He had done it himself. Mary might forgive, but she could never forget.

So he let the dreams go. They no longer mattered. All that mattered now was redemption. And here, perhaps, was the place to win it.

The sweat crept from under Hatch's hat and trickled down his face, burning his eyes, carrying the taste of salt to his lips. The sand was stove-lid hot against his skin.

But his conscience was still. And Claude Hatch was smiling.

Espy Norwood had spoken few words since they had left Mobeetie, and none since they had found the first sign of the Arrowhead herd being driven westward. His face was rigid as stone.

Beside him rode the sheriff and Sam Kirk, and behind him a dozen Figure 4 cowboys, as well as several townsmen and friends of Arch McCavitt who had declared themselves in. Altogether there were twenty men.

Espy rode like a man in a trance, a wall built around himself. He heard nothing, felt nothing, saw nothing.

He had driven himself without mercy, trying hard not to think, knowing that if he *did* think, he couldn't go through with it.

Sam Kirk jerked his horse to a halt. "Did you hear that?"

Espy had heard nothing. But now he did hear it. Distant gunfire.

Then the sheriff pointed. "Look yonder. Somebody's coming on horseback, and in a hurry to."

The lone rider evidently saw the group of horsemen. He immediately swung their way. Watching him, Espy realized it wasn't a man. Too small.

Suddenly his breath stopped. Could it be . . .

Yes! By George, it *was—Kenny!*

Espy jabbed spurs to the horse's sides. He was fifty yards in the lead when he reached the boy, slid to a stop, and jumped to the ground. He grabbed Kenny out of the saddle and crushed the boy to him, closing his eyes against the sudden burning. He tried to say something to his son, but his throat was choked tight. He just held him a long moment, making no further effort to speak.

In high excitement, Kenny blurted his story. From far across the hill an occasional shot still echoed.

"Come on," Espy said, "let's try to help Hatch."

But the gunfire stopped before they reached the creek. Espy exchanged glances with Sam Kirk. They knew.

Two riders pulled up out of the creek bed. They stopped and stared in consternation at the twenty horsemen. Then they turned and dropped back out of sight.

The sheriff made a sweeping motion with his arm. The posse spread out in a wide fan-shape movement and closed in upon the creek. Espy stayed in the center. When a bullet picked up dust in front of his horse, he touched spurs and made a dash for cover.

His mount hit the bank and slid down. Espy caught a glimpse of a tall man with a scar face and triggered a shot at him. The tall man broke into a hard run down the dry creek bed, where one of the other possemen was sure to get him.

Another bullet thumped into the dried bank beside Espy, sending a shower of sand into Espy's face. He jumped free of the saddle, turning the horse loose and diving belly-down beneath a cedar. The gunman was behind a cottonwood on the other side of the gravelly bed. Espy fired once. His shot was quickly answered. The man was a good marksman, for the bullet sliced through cedar leaves just above Espy's head.

There was only one way to get him. Espy had to reach the other side—get to the top of the bank.

He fired once more at the cottonwood, then sprang up and pelted across the gravel. He felt something tug at his pants leg and burn his skin. He dived headlong behind a smaller cottonwood and lay there a moment, getting his breath back. He looked above him. The bank wouldn't be hard to scale, but he would be exposed to fire while he was climbing.

He took a deep breath and jumped for it. He heard one shot . . . two. Then he was on the bank.

Crouching, he ran toward the cottonwood behind which the gunman had hidden. For a second, as he looked down over the bank, he saw nothing. Then the gunman raised up. They saw each other at the same instant. Both men's guns swung around, and two gunshots echoed down the creek bed, one a split second ahead.

Espy gripped his gun for another shot. But it was unnecessary. Matt Ollinger stumbled down the steep bank and pitched forward. He rolled over once and lay still.

In a few minutes the possemen had all gathered.

With them was the tall outlaw, his hands tied to his saddle horn. Solemnly Sam Kirk motioned to Espy.

"I've found Claude Hatch," he said. "He's over here."

Hatch lay on his stomach behind a cut section of bank where he had made his stand. His cartridge belt lay before him, the loops empty. Espy lifted the gun from his limp hand and checked the cylinder. He shook his head.

"Not a single one left, Sam. He stayed with it right to the last."

Sam nodded gravely. "He always wanted to be somebody big. But he just didn't have the stuff."

Espy said, "You're wrong, Sam. He had the stuff. This is the biggest thing a man could do."

XX

FAR OFF on the right flank, Quirt Wolford had followed the Arrowhead herd, vengeance-lust burning relentlessly in him. A hundred times his right hand had felt for the gun that ought to be on his hip. His fist would knot, and a dry curse would well up. They wouldn't get away with it. He'd get a gun somewhere, and he'd get his chance. He'd see Matt Ollinger and the rest over the sights of it before he was done.

If only it wasn't for this damned left arm, this swollen, blackening arm that raged with the fires of hell.

Wolford's lips were dry and cracked with fever. A sickening red haze obscured whatever he looked at, and it was getting worse. He was starving for water—he'd trade half that herd for a full canteen. And this aching, the godawful throb that jarred his whole body—he'd sell his soul to rid himself of it before it drove him out of his mind.

He watched the approaching riders for a full minute before the meaning of what he saw hammered through to his fevered brain. He saw confusion strike the outlaws at the herd. One of them fired at the posse before it was within range. The rest of them waited no longer. They abandoned the cattle and ran.

Wolford reined up in a low swale and watched. He saw the posse gradually eat up the distance and take in the rustlers one by one. There was no shooting. Not a man put up any resistance when he saw he was caught.

Wolford watched, and he began to laugh. It was a

wild, high, wheezing laugh born of a fever-crazed mind.

Laughing, he leaned over too far. He made a grab at the saddle horn—too late. The ground rushed up toward him. He landed with full weight on the poisoned, rotting arm. A cry of anguish tore from deep within him, and a spinning pool of darkness swam up to meet him.

With a supreme effort he managed to raise up onto his knees, and finally to his feet. He swayed like a drunken man. A searing lance thrust through his body, again and again and again. He stumbled forward, toward his horse. The animal shied, pricking its ears at him, but it didn't run. Catching the reins, he tried twice to shove his foot into the stirrup before he finally made it. It took all the courage he could muster to pull himself into the saddle. He took a tight grip on the horn this time. The world was spinning crazily.

Fear began to take hold of him. If he ever fell off again, he knew, he could never get back into the saddle. He'd walk and stumble and fall down and die.

The agony of the arm was getting worse. A doctor! He had to have a doctor. What good was freedom if a man was dead? He had to do something about that arm.

His vision was failing him, but he still knew directions. He reined the horse around and headed him back. He'd find Mobeetie. He *had* to get to Mobeetie.

How he finally got there, he didn't know. Part of the time he'd been out of his head, his fever-racked body leaning heavily over the horn. How many hours or days he'd been, he could not know. But one thing he did know. That was Mobeetie ahead.

The sight of it cleared his head. Caution. He had to use caution.

He knew where the doctor lived, in a two-room

adobe house. Wolford picked it out and guided the horse toward it. Warily he watched for sign of people. They wouldn't take him. He wouldn't let them take him.

He saw the water barrel at the back door. Thirst was a living devil in his parched throat, driving him wild. He eased down from the saddle, groaning at the knifing pain. He stumbled toward the barrel—shoved his face into it. The cool taste of the water almost made him fall unconscious again. He straightened, holding the edge of the barrel until he had steadied. Then he leaned over and drank slowly.

The effect of the water was almost miraculous. His vision cleared. He could stand now and not sway so much. He could walk without stumbling.

But that arm still throbbed, a steady, driving, crazing pain.

He walked around the house and pounded on the door. A Mexican boy with a broom in his hand finally opened it.

"Doctor . . ." Wolford said, ". . . got to see the doctor."

The boy's brown eyes widened qualmishly at the sight of Wolford's swollen, blackened arm. *"No está—no está."*

"Where is he?" Wolford grabbed the kid desperately and shook him with his good hand. "Where is he?"

The frightened youngster pointed toward the back end of a frame saloon a hundred yards away— McCavitt's saloon. *"Es con Señor McCavitt. En la cantina."*

Through the open door Wolford saw a gun belt hanging on the wall. He shoved inside, grabbed the belt and yanked it down from the peg. The boy, boogered

like a jackrabbit, darted past him and out the door.
Wolford yelled, but he couldn't catch him.

He lurched through the door and back outside. He
moved heavily toward the saloon.

At the rear of the building he paused uncertainly,
wondering which of the two doors to try. There was a
window. He squinted painfully, trying to see outside.

He saw a man lying on a bed, still and quiet, as if
asleep. A girl sat watching. A second man was cutting
white cloth with a big pair of scissors. Wolford got it
through his brain that this man was cutting a bandage.
He must be the doctor.

Wolford tested the doorknob. Shoving the door
open, he drew the gun and stumbled inside.

The doctor and the girl stared in surprise. The girl
started to stand up. Wolford waved the gun at her.
"Keep still."

The doctor's eyes dropped to Wolford's bad arm. In
shock, his lips moved with words unsaid.

"You're coming with me, Doc," Wolford said. His
voice was labored and thick. "My arm . . . you got to
treat my arm."

The doctor laid the scissors on the edge of the bed
and moved cautiously toward Wolford. "My God,
man," he said quietly, "that arm . . . You can't go
anywhere."

"Got to get away. Go west. You'll go with me. Take
care of my arm."

The doctor nodded toward Arch McCavitt, who lay
pale and still on the bed. "I can't leave here. This man
needs me, just as you do. If I leave, he may die."

Wolford exploded. "To hell with him. You got to
go!"

He waved the gun. The doctor paled.

The girl stood up with hatred in her eyes. "If you

take the doctor, you'll surely kill Arch. And if you do that, I'll kill *you*, Wolford.''

He ignored her. "You coming, Doc?"

The doctor nodded hopelessly. "Very well."

Suddenly he tensed. The clatter of hoofs sounded on the street out front. There was a shuffle of feet in the saloon.

''What's that?'' Wolford demanded.

The girl listened a moment, then smiled triumphantly. "The posse," she said. "It's come back."

Wolford heard the clump of boots and the jingle of spurs on the wooden sidewalk out front. They came through the front door. He heard someone say, "Howdy, Norwood. Any luck?"

The footsteps kept coming toward the door.

Wolford stiffened. Norwood! Gone now was his desperate desire for escape. It was swallowed up in a blinding surge of hatred. Norwood! It was Norwood who had ruined him, who had destroyed all Wolford had built. Now Norwood was coming, and Wolford was waiting for him. His hand tightened on his gun. He edged carefully to the back wall, where he could face the door, where he could get a clear shot. He waited there, his lips flat against his teeth, his eyes aflame.

''Don't move, either one of you," he gritted. "Do and I'll kill you."

The door opened, and he squeezed the trigger.

Disappointment had a bitter taste for Espy Norwood, riding back to town with part of the posse. Sure, the race was over and the fight was won. Even now, some of the Figure 4 cowboys were driving the Arrowhead herd back to its home range. And Quirt Wolford's men rode with the posse, hands tied to their saddle horns.

Best of all, Kenny Norwood rode beside his father.

Kenny hadn't been hurt, so far as Espy could see. Mistreated, yes, but not hurt.

Even so, disappointment's keen edge cut at Espy. Quirt Wolford had gotten away.

He wouldn't get far. That's what his own men had said. Might even be dead already. But that wasn't the way Espy had wanted it. Not the way at all.

As the posse rode into Mobeetie, people gathered to watch. Down the crooked street, Espy could see a crowd in front of the hotel.

Sam Kirk pulled in beside him. "Mary's down there, and the directors too. Want to go on and give them the whole report?"

Espy shook his head. "You go, Sam. You tell them. You'd better tell Mary about her uncle, too.

"What're you going to do, Espy?"

"I'll be down after a bit. I want to stop off and see about Arch."

Kenny reined up with him. Espy said, "You go on with Sam, son. Saloon's no place for you. Not even Arch's."

He tied his horse to the hitchrack. He paused at the open door to take off his hat and sleeve the sweat from his face. Thunder, but he was dirty. Three days' beard, three days' dust. And tired—he could sleep a week.

"Howdy, Norwood," the bartender spoke. "Any luck?"

Espy nodded wearily. He walked on back toward Arch's room. The saloon was quiet, for its few customers stood outside, watching the posse move on down the dusty street. He shoved open the door.

The porcelain knob shattered under his hand.

Espy stumbled backward as the roar of gunfire shook the walls. He glimpsed the man who faced him. Then

he leaped aside as Wolford fired again. Espy's hand
went down and came up with a gun.

"Norwood!" There was no mistaking Wolford's
voice, even though it sounded tight with pain. "Norwood, throw your gun in here."

Espy did not.

"Throw it in here," Wolford gritted again, "or I'll
shoot the man on the bed."

Espy pitched the gun into the room. He knew what
was coming now.

"Now walk on in here!"

Espy's stomach went weak. A long time since he
had known fear like this, fear for himself. But it was
here now, his heart hammering, his breath short and
painful. He wondered if any man could ever walk into
the jaws of death and not feel the awful squeeze of fear.

With short, halting steps, Espy walked through the
door. He faced Quirt Wolford, and he was not ready for
what he saw. Wolford was a crazy man. His fevered
black eyes tried hard to focus on Espy. His right hand
was shaky on the gun. And his left . . .

Espy went sick at the sight of it, the smell of it.

Wolford laughed crazily. His hand steadied, tightening on the gun. Espy's breath stopped. He braced
himself.

Lilybelle moved so swiftly that Espy barely saw her.
Her slender right hand darted downward. The long steel
scissors flashed silver as she brought them up.

Wolford screamed.

The gun slanted toward the girl. Wolford's lips tightened as he tried hard to level it at Lilybelle.

Espy dived for his own gun, on the floor. He scooped
it up and shot fast.

The muzzle of Wolford's weapon tipped downward.
It slipped from his fingers and fell to the floor. Wolford
sighed, swayed forward, and rolled over on his face.

Lilybelle's cheeks drained white in horror. She
hirled away, falling across Arch and weeping bitter-
.

Espy began to get his breath again. He wiped the cold
veat from his face and walked shakily to the girl. He
aced his hands on her heaving shoulders.

"It's all right now," he whispered. "It's all right.
ou gave me the break I needed. Everything's all
ght."

She sobbed. "It was terrible . . . terrible."

"Sure," Espy said. "But it's over. All over."

Abruptly she stopped crying. She raised up, her eyes
ide. "Espy! Doctor! Come look!"

Arch was beginning to stir. His eyelids fluttered.
The gunfire. It had shaken him out of his coma, Espy
new.

Painfully, a little at a time, Arch opened his eyes. It
ok him a minute to begin to see. By that time the room
as full of people who had crowded in to find out what
e shooting was about. But the only thing Arch saw
as Lilybelle, standing over him, her white fingers
ripping his hand. Arch's face creased with a smile.

"I sure never figured I'd get to heaven." His voice
as weak, but the life was there.

Lilybelle squeezed his red-whiskered face between
er hands and kissed him softly. She was sobbing
gain, but this time it was different.

When he could, Espy told him, "She hasn't left you
wo minutes since we brought you in here, Arch. You
etter marry that girl."

Arch looked softly at her. Weakly he raised his hand
nd touched her honey-colored hair.

"I'm figuring on it," he said.

The best place the syndicate directors could find for a
oard meeting room was the dining room of the hotel.
hey used it.

Determinedly Mary Bowman stood before them an
restated her promise. "We'll start a roundup im
mediately. We'll get a full and accurate count. If the
syndicate's share isn't there, I'll turn back as many o
the Arrowhead cattle as I have to. I'll make the coun
good."

They had asked her to leave them then, so they coul
discuss the matter freely.

Now she was at the Lee & Reynolds store, making
provisions for the supplies the Figure 4 would need i
its roundup. Espy and Sam helped her.

Sam said, "Don't you worry, Mary. We'll build the
Figure 4 back to what it was. You just wait and see."

Mary shook her head. "Not *we*, Sam. I'm leaving
the Figure 4 as soon as the count is done and we'v
squared things up."

Sam was incredulous. "Leaving?"

Her voice was pinched with sadness. "I couldn't g
on living there, Sam. Not after all that's happened. I'l
move to the Arrowhead. It's not big, but it's mine. I'l
make a ranch out of it someway."

Worriedly Sam said, "I'm afraid, Mary, that you'r
going to have to cut the Arrowhead herd plenty deep i
you make your promise good. Fact is, there won't b
much left of it."

Her lips were tight. "Then I'll do the best I can wit
what I *do* have. I'd rather have a ranch with no cattle o
it than to keep what isn't mine."

Espy was standing outside the hotel, waiting, whe
the directors finally broke up their session. The lawye
Slagel came out scowling. His jaw was swollen. H
caught Espy glancing at him, and he glowered darkly
He strode away, fiercely swinging his cane.

The colonel slapped a heavy hand to Espy's shoul
der. He was grinning broadly, the way he had used t
do.

"Well, Espy," he said, "we won. We whipped Slagel's ears down. The syndicate's keeping its money in the Figure 4. In fact, we've decided to see what we can do about buying or leasing the land."

Espy grinned. "Congratulations, Colonel."

The old man's brown eyes danced in triumph. "It was Mary Bowman that did it, Espy. She had them eating right out of her hand. She's a little princess, that girl is."

Then he said, "They left me in full charge, Espy. I'm going to need a a permanent manager on the Figure 4. What do you say?"

Espy shook his head. "Thanks, Colonel. But I can't take it."

Judkins's thick eyebrows arched. "What's the matter? Have you got another job lined up?"

"You might call it that, I guess. But don't you worry about a manager. Go talk to Sam Kirk, Colonel. You won't find a better man."

The colonel nodded thoughtfully. "I'll talk to him, Espy. But what are you going to do?"

Espy grinned. "I'm going to try to marry a princess."

The afternoon sun was a bright gold memory, and the fiery red was slowly bleeding out of the clouds that hovered low over the hills to the west. Mary Bowman and Espy Norwood walked arm in arm out past the Figure 4 saddle shed. They stopped to watch while Jess Cooley bolted a chuckbox to a wagon bed and tried at the same time to tell Kenny Norwood how to hold a rope.

Joe Kirk cast a quick loop at a cow skull nailed to a wooden keg. He caught it. Kenny tried and missed.

Jess called, "Now, Kenny, do like I told you. Don't hold the rope so close to the loop. Back your hand up a little. That's it. Now swing it over your head till it feels right, then throw it just like you'd throw a rock.''

Kenny did. And this time he caught. Jess hollered. ''That's the ticket. By the time this roundup is over, I'll have you almost as good a roper as I am. *Almost.*''

Espy chuckled, and Mary Bowman smiled. They walked on up the slope.

Mary said. ''Kenny's doing fine. I was afraid what he's been through might hurt him. But it doesn't seem to have bothered him much.''

Espy shook his head.

Mary said. ''The cowboys have all taken a liking to him. He'll have a lot of good teachers.''

Espy nodded seriously. ''Yes. but he needs a mother.''

Her eyes lifted questioningly. Espy tried to go on with what he wanted to say. It wouldn't come out. They stood together in silence by Frank Bowman's spring, watching the water gush out and splash down the hillside.

''In a way, Espy,'' Mary said, ''I'm going to hate to leave all this. It's been a part of me, and I've been a part of it for so long. It's always hard to break away from the things that bind you to the past.''

Espy knew. He'd been through it. It had taken years for him to break away. But he had done it. And now he was free.

''Mary,'' he told her, ''the colonel offered me the managership if I'd stay. I turned him down.''

She looked at him in surprise. ''Why?''

''You're starting a new ranch, Mary. You'll need a manager.''

Her hand tightened on his. ''Thanks, Espy. But what good is a manager when I don't have any cattle?''

Espy said, ''Mary, I've been saving money for a long time. I've got a good-sized account stashed away in a Kansas City bank. And the colonel has promised to get me as much more as I need.

"I'd like to stock that ranch for you. I'll furnish the cattle, you furnish the land. We can work out a partnership. What do you say?"

She said what he had wanted to say, when he didn't have the words. "I'll do it on one condition, Espy. This will have to be a lifetime partnership—all the way!"

He reached for her. She came with face upturned, and they sealed the contract.

★★★★★★★★★★★★★★★★★★★★

The Biggest, Boldest, Fastest-Selling Titles in Western Adventure!

★★★★★★★★★★★★★★★★★★★★

CHARTER'S MOST WANTED LIST

Frank Bonham
_07876-1	BREAK FOR THE BORDER	$2.50
_77596-9	SOUND OF GUNFIRE	$2.50

Giles A. Lutz
_34286-8	THE HONYOCKER	$2.50
_88852-6	THE WILD QUARRY	$2.50

Will C. Knott
_29758-7	THE GOLDEN MOUNTAIN	$2.25
_71146-4	RED SKIES OVER WYOMING	$2.25

Benjamin Capps
_74920-8	SAM CHANCE	$2.50
_82139-1	THE TRAIL TO OGALLALA	$2.50
_88549-7	THE WHITE MAN'S ROAD	$2.50

Available at your local bookstore or return this form to:

CHARTER
THE BERKLEY PUBLISHING GROUP, Dept. B
390 Murray Hill Parkway, East Rutherford, NJ 07073

Please send me the titles checked above. I enclose _____ Include $1.00 for postage and handling if one book is ordered; 25¢ per book for two or more not to exceed $1.75. California, Illinois, New Jersey and Tennessee residents please add sales tax. Prices subject to change without notice and may be higher in Canada.

NAME _____

ADDRESS _____

CITY _____ STATE/ZIP _____

(Allow six weeks for delivery.)